RETRIBUTION

ALSO BY T. G. AYER

Young Adult Paranormal

THE VALKYRIE SERIES

Dead Radiance

Dead Radiance Audio

Dead Embers

Dead Embers Audio

Dead Chaos

Dead Chaos Audio

Dead Wrath

Dead Silence

Joshua - Dead Radiance

Joshua II - Dead Embers

Joshua III - Dead Chaos

Joshua IV - Dead Wrath

Joshua V - Dead Silence

THE HAND OF KALI SERIES

Fire & Shadow

Blood & Gold

Time & Fate

Fury & Virtue

Spirit & Soul

THE DARKWORLD ORIGINS

Pyros (Logan)
Ailuros (Kailin)

~

THE DARK SIGHT SERIES

Dark Sight
Cursed Sight
Vissarion
Shadow Sight
Dark Prophecy
Cursed Prophecy
Shadow Prophecy

~

THE APSARA CHRONICLES

Immortal Bound
Gods Ascendent
Dominion Falling
Vengeance Born
Last Legion

~

A SEASON OF ASH AND BONE

Heartfyre

~

Adult Sci-Fi

HANDS ASSASSIN

Death Dealer

Death Mark

Death Strike

Hand's Assassins Series

~

NEW ADULT CONTEMPORARY THRILLER W/A TONI VALLAN

Beautiful Collision

Beautiful Conviction

~

PSYCHOLOGICAL HORROR W/A TONI VALLAN

Dark Shadows

Splinter

Retribution
The Irin Chronicles #1

Cover art by Eduardo Priego
Editor: J.C. Hart
ISBN-10: 0473429233
ISBN-13: 978-0473429232

Retribution

USA TODAY BESTSELLING AUTHOR

T.G. AYER

The DarkWorld Universe, currently the SkinWalker Series and the SoulTracker series also includes the Irin Chronicles. The Irin Brotherhood act under a veil of secrecy, and have done so for centuries. The various councils within the DarkWorld are aware of the existence of the Irin operatives but the regular guy on the street has no clue.

So Kailin and Logan, Melisande and Saleem, and the rest of the characters from the DarkWorld—who you have probably already met—are going about their merry way with no clue that Evie and her team are also working to keep the world safe.

As yet, their paths have not crossed, but they do later in the series.

If you haven't picked up the SkinWalker or SoulTracker books yet, you may want to start with Skin Deep to get a feel for the Universe.

Alternatively, you could read Irin 1 & 2 and then run through the other DarkWorld books bearing in mind that both the Skin-Walker and the SoulTracker series have active crossover scenes.

There will be more to come in the DarkWorld Universe—DeathTalker and the Iron Queen likely to be one of the first to be released in the next year, telling the characters' stories from their own points of view, and shining a light on who they are and what their own lives look like.

T.G. Ayer
    The DarkWorld

CHAPTER 1

Evangeline ducked into the shadows as Baltazar crossed the street. When he reached the sidewalk, he glanced over his shoulder and stared straight at her. Evie silenced a gasp. For the briefest second, she feared she'd been spotted.

Then he turned, looked ahead and continued walking.

Evie remained steeped in darkness until she felt assured he wouldn't be turning around to investigate the shadows.

The Boston night was cold. Icy enough to snare her breath and weave misty coils with it in the air before her face. But she paid scant attention to the weather. She had followed Marcellus' directions and arrived at the demon's lair. Her search had come up with nothing, so she had followed Baltazar hoping the object the Master was after was on the demon's person. She had tracked him through the warren of old, red-brick Colonial buildings along Acorn Street and its narrow cobbled roads. She was careful to soften the sound of her heels on the smoothed stones. Hugged by fresh green moss, the worn stones shone in the pale moonlight, brightening the street. But the iridescent beauty of the multi-hued, red-and-grey cobblestones was lost on Evie.

It only put her on edge.

She kept her eyes on Baltazar's muscle-bound shoulders, stalking him as he loped to the edge of a small tree-lined park which hugged the darkened neighborhood. Old gas lamps cast pale, buttery light on his dark head as he walked the stone pathway that curved through the elms and oaks. He was large with the body of a wrestler and limbs and muscles to match. But that didn't matter to Evie.

He was no match for her.

Baltazar slipped through an opening in the tree-line up ahead and disappeared down the hillside without a sound. Evie followed, avoiding branches and shrubbery as adeptly as her quarry. She tailed him until he arrived at a cliff-top clearing that gave a glittering, magical view of the city.

Tiny pinpricks of lights flickered and blinked in the valley below, like multi-colored diamonds thrown carelessly on the dark surface of the land.

While the view held his attention, Evie bent and drew her silver dagger from her boot, releasing her Damascus blade from its leather sheath. She held her breath, weighing both blades in her hands, gaining comfort and strength from their familiar weight.

She was ready.

Evie, coming up behind him, closed the distance between herself and the demon Baltazar, silent as a leopard stalking its oblivious prey. Her feet whispered over the dew-kissed grass. So light was her step she may as well have floated across the small field.

Trees sighed behind her in a deceivingly gentle breeze. Evie drew closer—just close enough that an obliging gust would carry her scent to him.

She counted the seconds under her breath.

His back stiffened, his neck muscles rigid as he turned so

slowly she could almost see the hair on his skin undulate as he moved.

Her scent evoked similar reactions with all her marks. The perfume of death, their very own Reaper come to call. And she never tarried with them. Social niceties somehow seemed out of place where knives and blood and imminent death were intertwined. Besides, these creatures wallowed so far beneath her on the moral and genetic ladder as to be untouchable, unworthy.

Baltazar swallowed.

The tendons in his neck remained taut as bowstrings. Then he drew a ragged breath and opened his mouth. He may have intended to ask her a question. Something typically innocuous. A ridiculous gesture as none of their questions received an answer —if they ever got the chance to ask one.

The demon didn't.

In a swift and viciously smooth swipe of her left hand, Evie plunged the silver dagger deep into his chest, so deep only the carved hilt prevented farther penetration. The slim blade embedded itself securely within his heart, flaying open arterial walls, penetrating the center of his demonic soul. Creatures of the Underworld had a seething dislike for anything silver. Perhaps it was the metal's innate ability to end their miserable lives. The accuracy of her aim was helped by the conveniently human location of his heart.

She followed quickly with her right hand, sweeping the curved blade of the Damascus dagger clean across his throat. The deadly edge slid smoothly through glamor, demon hide, and bone.

Quick. Clean.

Landing in a crouch, Evie held her breath and watched him through the strands of her hair, which had escaped its bindings at the back of her head. It had happened so fast. Too quickly for the demon to defend himself. His body fell slowly, crumpling awkwardly onto his back until he landed beside her. Evie met his eyes. And sucked in a breath, an unconscious pause as she waited to see the last emotions fly across the demon's face.

Always, she watched the last light in the eyes of her mark flicker and fade. She'd made herself do that whenever it was possible to be sure she never lost sight of the significance of her job. Evie had witnessed final moments of pure rage and comical disbelief. As a warrior of the Irin, she'd been doing Marcellus' bidding for six months now, and she'd begun to notice a pattern to the behaviors of her targets. They were always pissed when they got caught and always a little more than upset to find their existence about to be permanently terminated.

This last one was different, though. This time, what she saw planted a tiny seed of doubt within the darkest recesses of her mind. His eyes were the palest of blues. It held anger and annoyance. But she also saw confusion and disbelief that faded as his life dissipated.

Soon, wracking her mind, trying get a bead on the strange feeling that was so elusive, she stood over dancing amber embers flickering over the grass in the night breeze. The rising ashes and slivers of dust caught the next swift breeze and rode the night wind in silence. If she had learned anything in her long lifetime, she knew better than to ignore her instincts.

She scowled.

Something was wrong.

Baltazar had been too easy to track. And she had taken his ignorance of her presence for arrogance. A nonchalance that spoke of a self-assured killer, but killers often got sloppy in their arrogance. They get careless, cocky. She had paused a few times to wonder if she had mixed up the scents. No. He had been the right mark.

Now she stared down at the last of the fading embers.

Soon, there was nothing but the glistening, almost-black blood that marred the slim, deadly beauty of her Damascus blade and the silver face of the dagger that had pierced his heart. As she bent to wipe her blade off on a nearby patch of grass, she neither mourned nor regretted her actions.

This was just a job.

The very act of wiping the blood off the blades was purely habit. She knew, as well as any other hunter of her ilk, that the essence of a demon's life force was destroyed when they were killed. For some unknown, and on her part unquestioned, reason, the Creator of these creatures did not wish the world tainted by their lifeless remains. Few people knew where these creatures went in their afterlife.

These demons she killed, they were nothing. Murderers. Evil.

Evie just seemed to be in the garbage business lately.

So why was it bothering her more and more each day. Why did she feel a sense of wrong each time she killed a mark? Was it their human glamors that had gotten to her? That they lived a pretense of normal human lives to hide their true nature? Was it that before Marcellus she'd never belonged to a demon death squad? Or was it that she just missed doing good?

She stood over the grassy spot where the blades were still bent at unnatural angles, having been crushed beneath Baltazar's weight. Of all the possessions left of him, it was a metal disk which had caught and held her attention. Only moments ago, it had hung on a fat bronze chain around the demon's neck. Thick, heavy and ornately carved with tiny swirls and patterns, its surface gleamed in the moonlight.

Evie picked up the disc, feeling the solid weight of it in her palm. She frowned, trying to concentrate, but she quickly gritted her teeth, admitting she was unable to identify the language. But even as she did, she knew the script was beyond her knowledge. She'd have to wait to take it home.

Frustrated, she glanced around the deserted clearing. Nobody would have seen her. She'd cast a glamor around herself and threw angel-light around her—standard protocol on a mission.

Hidden within the blanket of her glamor, Evie wasted precious time studying the strange piece.

Octagonal in shape, the disk bore a small carving on each of the eight corners. A hole bored through the center and inscriptions covered the back. The tiny carvings resembled Greek or Roman, possibly Persian, figures. An impressive relic.

A sudden sound interrupted her thoughts. She breathed again. Just a car backfiring. But it was enough to remind Evie of her duties.

Whether demon or human, the dead didn't take anything with them.

Evie gathered the other solid items from the grass and threw them into a small envelope, which she hurriedly stuffed into her bag. Jewelry, belt buckles, and the odd spur or two needed to be rounded up from the scene. In the past she, would have dumped the remaining trinkets she'd found. Not in the last six months though. Marcellus had given them all strict instructions to ensure every piece of metal be brought to him. No questions. Marcellus certainly had a different method of running the Irin than Patrick. None of the teams enjoyed the feeling of being under his control.

Most of all Evie.

She clenched her fist. It was time to leave. Not that she feared being tracked, nor did she waste time worrying over being observed making a kill. She was too good at her job. It just annoyed her that she couldn't put a finger on what bugged her about this whole kill.

Something feels off.

Everything in order, she swept her eyes over the scene. One last check didn't hurt. Satisfied, she was about to take off when a ray of light bounced off something in the taller grass at the edge of the clearing. Her night vision was superb, so she admonished herself for not finding it on her first scan of the area.

But when she looked closer, she saw it had been half hidden by a fallen branch. She strode over to the grass, bent to retrieve the trinket, and felt its weight immediately. The ring that lay in the palm of her hand looked ancient. Possibly Minoan from the carving and the color of the gold. What would a low-life, albeit high-level, demon be doing with an ancient artifact like this? Another little piece to add to the puzzle slowly growing around Baltazar's untimely end.

Evie sighed and unfolded her wings. They stood a head taller than her, beautiful, pearly white and iridescent under the moonlight. Her angelic heritage had failed to bestow upon her all its glorious abilities, and so she could not disapparate to the Irin HQ, but she needed to calm herself anyway. Flying always gave her a sense of peace she could not find in anything else she did. She strengthened the glamor over herself, making her invisible to any eye that may be cast heavenward.

Flexing and spreading wide, her wings lifted her up into the night sky. Toward the twinkling stars. Toward peace, silence, and calm.

"IT IS DONE!" Daniel Feinstein stared at the list of names inked onto the ancient parchment. The relic lay dry and brittle beneath his sweaty fingers, waiting for the slightest change heralding Evangeline's latest successful termination.

"She has terminated Baltazar.... This is good. Is it confirmed?" Seated calmly behind the heavy oak desk, Master Marcellus waited for Daniel's confirmation. The Master's black garb, as nondescript as the next Brother, did nothing to mark him as one apart from the group, above the rest in any way. Yet a dark air remained around him, shadowing him. Marking him as different.

In addition, the previous Master, Patrick had conveniently fallen victim to a long and untimely illness. Despite his immortality, he had been unable to overcome the strangely inexplicable affliction. As Patrick's successor, it made perfect sense for the right hand of the old Master to take his place. Master Marcellus

Bactor smiled to himself, taking comfort in his position of power. The Brotherhood still answered to him with the same reverence bestowed upon their previous leader.

Daniel stared at the name "Baltazar" etched in ageless ink in an ancient and forgotten language. Progress dragged slowly, and it would be a while yet before the rest of the Seals were gathered. Daniel gripped the fragile parchment a little too firmly. The crackle of the paper brought him back and he loosened his grip.

"Yes, his name has just disappeared from the list." Daniel glanced at Marcellus.

He considered Marcellus and his position within the Irin. With the power of the Nephilim at their fingertips, they were fast becoming invincible. Half-breed angels from the four corners of the globe. This kind of reach was unimaginable until the Irin Warriors proved their prowess. They were the best tools to obtain the Seals. Even better—they were dispensable.

Evangeline was on her way back. His eyes flicked toward the curtains framing the balcony. He could almost picture her there, blue eyes flashing, lustrous black hair framing a beautiful face. Yes, she had been blessed with angelic genes, so understandably she would have the face to prove it.

She always entered through those doors when she returned from a termination. He assumed it was a display of some kind. Power perhaps? To remind the simple humans of what she was. What she was capable of. Ignorant whelp. If she only knew who she was dealing with....

Daniel longed to teach her exactly where she belonged in the order of things. Sadly, she was the example by which many of the other Warriors marked themselves. She spelled trouble.

He returned to his desk, a smaller, messier version of the Master's antique.

A little restraint would go a long way. Alerting the Nephilim would be dangerous. Her vow was to serve the Brotherhood, to aid in wiping away the scourge of Hell seeping through the portals and worming its way into the human world. An unbreakable bond between Nephilim and Brotherhood. The Brotherhood of the Irin—they were Nephilim scouts or human agents who believed they served a higher purpose.

As did Evangeline.

CHAPTER 2

*E*vie approached the Irin Estate as darkness slipped from the sky and crimson fingers of sunlight scarred the farthest horizon, so red it reminded her of great splotches of blood.

She shuddered.

This job must be getting to her. Such morbid thoughts contradicted the exquisite beauty of the night's star-speckled heavens.

She dove, wings tucked close, glancing toward a balcony that skirted the roof of the East Wing. She came in for the landing, her pure-white, silver-tipped wings spread wide, slowing herself down as she approached the roof. She flipped her body upright and prepared to land nimbly on the balls of her feet. At the very last minute, she tucked in her wings, allowing her body to free-fall the last few feet. Evie dropped to the edge of the roof, landing in a crouch, ready to defend herself, prepared to fight. She stayed low, resting her elbow on one knee and scanned the rooftop.

Her feet crunched against gravel. The rooftop was empty. Evie rose and walked to a parapet guarded by a pair of small concrete gargoyles sitting short and squat. They grimaced over the front gardens of the estate, their hooded eyes staring out into the dark, silent night. The estate lights threw little patches of glowing yellow patches outside a multitude of open doors and windows. The gardens beyond lay dark as pitch, though Evie was certain the Irin Night Guard lurked among the trees and shrubs. Yet no sound or movement indicated their presence. They were good.

A breeze rode the silent air, strong fingers that cooled the heat of her face. To her left, the pint-sized stone gargoyle still stared out across the gardens, indifferent to her presence. Concrete and plaster. A fake. Made to resemble the real thing in a time when people had long forgotten that gargoyles were living, breathing, feeling, and thinking creatures. She knew the gargoyle night watch was serious about security, patrolling the estate religiously. They were around, somewhere.

Another gust of wind. Awareness rippled along her skin and she turned slowly to her right, staring straight into the dark and watchful eyes of the real thing. The gargoyle guard was silent, his obsidian eyes dark and clear in his ebony face. He inclined his head slightly, acknowledging her, but still watchful, still on guard.

She was disappointed.

But she should have expected no more than the courteous greeting she received. She was Nephilim. Warrior of the Irin Brotherhood. Even Evie's friends frowned upon fraternizing with non-angelic beings.

Do your job. Kill the mark. Go straight home. Don't make friends. Irin monopoly at its very best.

Life was getting tedious these days. With Patrick ousted and Marcellus playing top dog, the changes wreaked havoc with their lives. The other Warriors became restless too. The new topic of conversation--between the morning's lessons or the afternoon's practice sessions in the armory--was Marcellus.

Marcellus was a volatile leader. He either instilled mortal fear in his followers or just plain rubbed them the wrong way. In a few short months since he'd taken over, he'd sent them chasing Earth-side demons and scrounging for random pieces of demon metal like a pack of scavenging hellhounds. He'd used genial smiles and subtle manipulation to ensure the Irin, masters and warriors alike, believed nothing but good about him. And the worst of it was many of the Irin masters had fallen for his charm.

Evie ground her teeth. What a waste of time. But she meant to make her report and get on with her day. She still had to rest and prepare for her morning classes. The Brotherhood ensured each Nephilim of similar age, along with various new recruits, attended the relevant classes. It was Patrick's idea to start the training center. He, more than any of the other Brothers, knew what the Nephilim went through. Because he had raised Evie and because he'd seen too much over his extended lifetime. He was convinced educating the Warriors would help them complete their assignments successfully. Their *education* covered everything from languages to history to politics. Patrick was nurturing a new breed of Irin Warriors. That was until Marcellus took charge. One of Evie's greatest fears was that the new Master would decide training was unnecessary.

A long, long lifetime did not necessarily mean a Nephilim received a proper education. In addition, their longevity did not mean they were endowed with adulthood automatically. Most of the Nephilim here at the center experienced tumultuous childhoods. A Nephilim aged in years like a human being from birth to puberty. Once the hormones kicked in, angel and human blood warred within body and mind. Until one won. Many Nephilim reverted to humanity, allowing their angelic natures to wilt like a plant deprived of water, never knowing what they'd missed out on. Never knowing they'd come so dangerously close to immortality.

For some, like Evie and the Warriors of the Irin, the angelic half won out. From then onward, aging was a wholly different process. Nephilim lived a few hundred years before they aged one human year. For a Nephilim, the teenage years lasted close to a thousand years before full maturity was achieved. For now, Evie was the human equivalent of nineteen, and she would stay nineteen for a good few years more. As long as she retained the company of her fellow Warriors, she could handle it.

A gust of wind buffeted her as she leapt over the parapet and floated slowly to the stone-tiled surface of the balcony. It ruffled her feathers, lifted and moved them with invisible fingers. She welcomed the touch, the warmth of Mother Nature against her body. Evie chose the balcony entrance for its proximity to the rooftop.

And because it affected Daniel.

Evie delighted in the definite wobble of his stiff upper lip whenever she made a balcony entrance. She suspected he didn't like her much. The feeling was certainly mutual.

Evie flung the doors open, slipping through the parting in the heavy brocade curtain into the dimly lit room. This was the center of operations of the Irin, a Brotherhood whose purpose was to serve the good of mankind, but the room held the air of an animal's den. A cool menace replaced the open care with which Master Patrick had led the teams. The Warriors shared a devotion to a cause they strongly believed in, and Patrick had been the home in which many Nephilim sought refuge. And his office had been their headquarters, their haven.

Marcellus had made changes. Changes he had intended to be subtle were anything but. He'd closed down offices of the Irin worldwide, put a freeze on new admissions, threatened to expel anyone who went against him and even prohibited the use of the Nephilim's special mind-reading powers. For members of the team who had been together for decades if not centuries, each change marked an end to an unforgettable era.

But the teams had no choice but to grit their teeth and bear the changes like scars on their skin. Master Patrick would be disappointed should they show any disrespect to his successor. The Brotherhood had conferred the title of leader to him when he had stood forward and claimed the right of Edis. Edis allowed a member of fellowship to place a vote for himself as the next Master, effectively a legal coup.

Evie steeled her features for the Master.

"Ah! My dear Evangeline. We've been expecting you." A ssmil--so near to sincere that the ice dwelling in his eyes could easily have been missed within the jolly creases of his grinning jowls--crossed his face.

With an expansive wave at an overstuffed couch, he invited her to sit. Evie refused as always.

Give him the opportunity to tower over me in some misguided sense of authority? Fat chance.

She stood. Through her lashes, she noticed the slightly raised eyebrows on Daniel's overstressed face. Noticed the barest tightening around the Master's mouth. Just a hint, not enough to reveal his real emotions.

"I see you have terminated the mark." His eyes grazed the packet she held.

A flick of her hand and the envelope sailed through the air, landing on the desk with a resounding thunk. He grimaced, and Evie could tell he used every ounce of his willpower to stop from checking for dents or damage to the ancient wood. Evie suppressed a smile. She was not the malicious type, but sometimes, just sometimes, it felt good to torment the Master.

Now Marcellus was watching her, his expression for a moment revealing a clear dislike, as if he thought of her as nothing more than an insolent brat in need of a good beating. But in that moment, she saw a flash of fear too—as if something held him back from lashing out at her insolence.

Evie gritted her teeth. This was taking too long. The sooner she left this room, the better for everyone. She suppressed a shudder. The lights were off and only two candles flickered in the darkened office. Marcellus had most likely intended for the shadows to intimidate her, the way they hugged the edges of the room, shielding the corners from easy perusal. Not for Evie though as she used her own personal brand of night-vision. God-given.

Something tugged at her awareness and she probed back. Yes, there it was in the darkest, farthest corner. A hazy shape wavered, blending into the shadows so well no human eye would ever have seen it.

A dark creature. Perhaps a shade or spirit of some sort.

Now what was a man of God doing associating with a creature of the Underworld?

Not that Evie or any of the Warriors believed there was a single decent bone in their new Master's body. She blinked, keeping her face and body as relaxed and unaffected as possible. They need not know she was onto them, and this was one piece of information to file away for the moment.

As Evie watched Marcellus, the air thickened with anticipation. His eye twitched in the direction of the night creature. Marcellus glanced back at Evie, drumming his fingers on the arm of his well-stuffed chair. *Concerned I may have seen your secret visitor?* But Evie feigned ignorance, turning away from the offending creature and inspecting the envelope that minutes ago was the center of the attention of all three of the room's occupants.

Living occupants, that is.

"So, another one bites the dust?" Evie commented drily.

"Well, we have terminated another lowlife and saved humanity from being terrorized by one of Satan's minions, if that's what you mean." Marcellus' words were cool and critical as if he sensed Evie's judgment. "Evangeline, you seem to have doubts, my dear. Let me assure you that we are contributing to the good of humanity. That is, of course, who we serve."

"You haven't explained the reasons for wanting these." She waved her hand over the buckles and piercings spilling from the now-open envelope. "The possessions of the marks? We used to throw them into the smelter so they can never be used again by another being with evil intentions. You know as well as I do that some demons' possessions retain the owner's power. Hugely unpredictable in the hands of an Innocent." Evie baited him.

Marcellus' decree that all metal objects found in the possession of any mark must be returned to him during debrief had become a concern for the teams and many of the other council members. The very act of collecting items of demonic power alerted the other Warriors to the possibility that the new Master intentions were questionable. So the Warriors completed each mission as prescribed and metal items returned to him as per instruction, but anything Evie thought was of any value she retained and hid away.

In the last few months, most of what he had seen were belt buckles, earrings, and boot spurs along with a small pile of tongue and lip piercings. Demons had a fetish for the human art of body piercings. And cowboy boots. Evie had no idea if any of the other Warriors had weakened to Marcellus' demands, but his arrogance was beginning to seep through his refined persona. Now was just such a time. False confidence with his shadow friend, seemingly hidden within the dark corners of the room?

His forehead bore the slightest of creases as he contemplated his next move. Evie could almost hear his thoughts. Had to concentrate to shut them out. Her power to delve into the minds of humans was an asset. But not here. Amongst the Irin, she was forbidden to listen.

Part of her vow as an Irin Warrior inhibited her use of her telepathic ability within the grounds of the Brotherhood compound. It was a weak pledge, but for the most part, the Nephilim behaved.

In light of the circumstances with Baltazar and now the unwelcome, underworldly visitor in the corner, Evie's vow proved very difficult to keep, especially when all she had to do was lift the veil the teensiest bit, just to hear a whisper of his thoughts.

No. She was stronger than her temptation. She had to find another way. Besides, who knew what magic he may have used to detect mindreading from the Nephilim.

Marcellus rose, veins pumping at his temple. It seemed the Master was forfeiting this round as he walked to the windows through which she had made her most bothersome entrance. It was his cue that he was done with her, for now.

Thrilled to leave, Evie exited the room, steeling herself from barging through the doors at a dead run.

CHAPTER 3

$\mathcal{E}$vie mulled over the meaning of the metal artifacts she'd retrieved from Baltazar. Barely rested, she headed to join the rest of the younger Nephilim for the morning sessions.

The sound of her heels on the floor changed from a soft patter on cool marble tile to a hollow clack on solid wood flooring and she found herself taking the main corridor to the West wing. Evie smiled. Her subconscious knew better what she needed. She had to see Master Patrick.

If the sound of Evie's feet on her journey had not roused her from her reverie, the odor of the Wing itself would have called her attention to direction and destination. The passage, lined with warm wood paneling at least two centuries old, gave off the aroma of "ancient." Mustiness clung from the beveled cornices of the ceilings, to the dust topping the curves of the wrought-iron lamps, and to the cobwebs, which swayed like little grey ghosts watching Evie pass. Ancient paintings of long-dead Irin Masters dotted the wall. Each face bore pained and long-suffering expressions as if they too could smell the odor and disapproved strongly.

The darkness and shadows oppressed Evie, and no magic was

allowed, even to brighten the passage. No outside light reached these halls, which added to the sense of entombment in a warren of dead Masters. Evie shivered. The dark corridors had never seemed oppressive or dank. Not until Marcellus moved in. He'd brought a darkness with him that filled the shadows with suspicion and a hint of evil.

She walked on, chiding herself for being paranoid, and turned a corner. The West Wing was well loved, well cared for. Except for this almost-forgotten end of it. Evie's heart turned painfully in her chest. And she tasted the bitter bile of hatred.

She had tried. But opposing Marcellus' new position because of her gut instinct hadn't been enough. Especially when Master Patrick had assured her Marcellus was true to the cause. But nothing sat right in Evie's gut when she looked at the new Master. It was as if even the marrow in her bones rebelled against his authority.

The tapping of her heels slowed to a halt as she came to the heavy oak door to Master Patrick's chambers. Patrick, relegated to the West Wing to live out the rest of his weak and ailing life, seemed to take it in his stride, with grace and dignity.

But it was a double blow for the Warriors. Despite the Council member's objections, Marcellus had been adamant that Patrick needed to recuperate in private.

Evie didn't believe it for one second. The Irin Estate was immense. Plenty of room for Master Patrick. Marcellus had an ulterior motive for hiding his ailing predecessor away from his most loyal followers, within the oldest part of the facility. Evie had to hand it to him. He was a master strategist.

EVIE KNOCKED FIRMLY. Turning the heavy brass knob, she pushed the door open a little. With his hearing steadily failing, he didn't always hear her knock. If he was asleep, she'd come back again later. Evie peered around the door at the monstrosity of a bed. She hated the thing about as much as Patrick cherished it. A dark, almost black, polished mahogany four-poster hung with blood-burgundy and green-striped brocade curtains. The bed sucked every bit of the energy from the room.

Patrick was not in the bed, so she stepped quickly into the room, steeling herself against racing inside to search him out. Heart thumping, she scanned the gathering shadows. And found him sitting at his small writing table within the light of the morning sun. It filtered weakly into the room, pale and golden.

Dust-fairies swirled around on the sunbeams. Tiny trills of laughter filtered to Evie's ears, and she smiled. They moved around her as she passed from shadow to light and toward her mentor. Patrick looked up as she stepped closer. The fairies watched her as they flitted about, letting her pass. As tiny as weightless grains of sand, they floated on the breeze her shifting body made as she walked through a stream of the laughing creatures. Then they were back to basking in the sunbeams, their attention to the angel only a temporary thing.

Patrick smiled and it deepened the wrinkles at the corners of his deep, cornflower-blue eyes. Evie teased him mercilessly that he would have made a great Pope since he looked the part. His smile brought life to a face dull and gray with his current illness and with age, which had only recently begun to reveal itself. Evie's heart ached with sadness. He had been the perfect Grand Master, his immortality only helping the success and solidity of the order. His own predecessors had been mortal, just as the rest of the current masters were. Patrick had used that as an excuse, saying perhaps it was time for humans to take charge of the Irin.

Evie smiled sadly as he held his gnarled, wrinkled hands out to her as she knelt beside him. "How are you, Evangeline?" His words scratched out, dusty, unused like his ink and quills, like the handmade parchment she'd sourced from the rarest suppliers that sat untouched on his desk, lit only by the sun's rays.

"I am well, Master," Evie answered, hiding a sad smile.

"Now, Evangeline. You know better than to lie to me." It was too easy to forget that the man who sat, glowing in the now brightening sunlight, had been a father to her. He'd always been able to tell when she was fibbing. They'd spent enough centuries together. Enough to learn more about each other than most normal families could learn in their short lifetimes.

Now, she dropped her eyes, unable to admit her concerns about Marcellus. "It's nothing, Master. I'll get over it."

But Patrick wasn't to be misled that easily. Evie watched him study her face. Knew before he opened his mouth what he would say. "Marcellus again?" His eyes were old, but still bright and fearless. His sigh was soft as she nodded. "Child, you have to give Marcellus a chance to prove his strength as a Grand Master. I can't be Master forever."

He leaned against the soft cushion of his chair back, as if tired of the world itself, and patted her hand. Evie bit her tongue against the accusation teetering at its tip, like a ripened fruit ready to burst. She'd voiced her suspicions to Patrick before. Suspicions about Marcellus' intentions where Patrick himself was concerned. But Patrick had merely batted the accusations away. 'How would Marcellus kill an Immortal without detection?' Patrick had asked, his disbelief so evident in his question. Patrick had insisted his no longer being Master had no impact on Council decisions and posed no threat to Marcellus' rule of the Brotherhood.

But Evie had to wonder if those words were just a front and if Patrick was just giving up. Was there something more going on here than what Evie could see? She clenched her jaw. Evie meant to find out no matter what Patrick said.

For now she studied Patrick's face, her anger rising within her, an unchecked tide. "He's canned your plans to allow Sofia to join the Brotherhood you know," Evie said, bitter and angry again. Sofia was a Nephilim and a friend. She'd applied to join the

Irin but had been refused by Marcellus because she'd once worked for the local Demon Chieftains. Patrick had overlooked it as mistakes of the past and had championed her application but Marcellus had felt otherwise and vetoed her entry.

A shadow of dark color rose in the old man's face and he seemed to war against his emotions for a moment. Evie was glad that at least that piece of information had elicited a deeper emotional reaction from him. Sofia's plight deserved it. Eventually he released his breath and sighed, his face drooping sadly.

"I changed what I could in my time, Evangeline," he said, shaking his head as he looked at Evie, his eyes cloudy and paler than just moments ago. "The Brotherhood is centuries old. Time moves faster than the Irin."

"But she was ready to enter the Order before Marcellus found out. He cancelled the ordainment without even telling her. What is she supposed to do now?" Evie took care to ensure she didn't raise her voice. Patrick wasn't the one who deserved her rage.

"She had petitioned only me and I have done what I can. If the Master of the Irin refuses to ordain her, I am powerless to change anything."

"That's exactly what I mean, Father." Her dislike for Marcellus was palpable and she had to restrain herself from a more vehement statement. "He has put a halt on as many of your projects as he can. He's even recalled the West Coast Cadre."

Patrick was startled enough to look at Evie with disbelief. The West Coast division was as important as their headquarters here at the estate. The West Coast Irin were their eyes and ears out there. The old man remained silent for a while, a look of quiet contemplation on his aged features. "He is the new Master, child. I cannot influence his hand in any way. He will change the Brotherhood and mold it as he sees fit. And even if you believe he is not what he seems, it will only be time that will reveal his intentions. In the meantime, all you can do is your job."

His hand was warm on Evie's head. In essence, she was still

very much the child at the father's feet. Her father had chosen with wisdom when he had placed Evie with Patrick. Patrick who'd been a knight in his time, who'd had the knowledge to oversee a Brotherhood, which had grown from a tiny flotilla to an armada of angelic Warriors. He'd fought for the inclusion of all winged Warriors, the Asgardian Valkyries and the Indian Apsaras among others. He'd been tireless in his raising of Evie, so determined, so dedicated.

Now there were only two things Evie could accuse him of—dismissing his ailing state of health, and refusing to listen to her suspicions of Marcellus. He gave Evie the impression he was strong in his belief that the Council had chosen wisely. He believed, too, that his illness seriously hampered his ability to lead the Irin.

Evie, on the other hand, was convinced Marcellus had a nefarious plan. Perhaps it was time to confide in Patrick. Tell him about the metal pieces they were constantly hunting for.

"May I ask one more question, Father?"

He nodded gravely.

"Aren't demons unable to take metal with them beyond the Veil?"

"That's right." He nodded again, a tiny frown of curiosity marring his pale forehead.

Evie forged ahead. "Would the Irin need the metal the demons hold for any purpose at all?"

Patrick was already shaking his head. "No. There's nothing the demons possess that can benefit the Brotherhood in any way. Why do you ask?" Now the frown was no longer mildly curious.

"No reason. Just a question." Evie wanted to think about Patrick's confirmation first. Find out a little more before she confided the whole story to the old Master. The very real possibility that Patrick may soon leave this world was something Evie preferred not to think about. She desperately needed to believe in his longevity. "How are you feeling today? Has Castor been to see you?"

"No better than yesterday, child. And yes, Castor's been and given me the rubs and the oils and whatever those potions are that he creates." Patrick made a face and Evie smiled. Castor was special to Patrick too. There was a strange silence as he paused, searching her face. "Evie, you must know I do not have much time left."

His tone was so matter-of-fact that for a moment she was lost for words. And before she found the strength to negate his statement he said, "No point in denying it. I am not long for this world."

"But why? How is this happening? You are Immortal. Centuries old!" Evie shook her head in disbelief, quivering with impotent rage. "This shouldn't be happening."

Patrick leaned forward and laid a hand to her cheek. "But it is happening. And I don't know how to stop it." Patrick regarded Evie with helpless eyes, his soft palm with its papery-thin skin cupping her face.

"Can't we find someone? Isn't there anyone who can help?" She grabbed his hand, careful to not hurt him.

"My dear child, if there were someone who could help me, they would have done so by now." He sighed, the ragged sound so tired and defeated, so soft Evie wondered if she'd imagined it. "Perhaps the Archangels could have helped. But I sealed my fate a thousand years ago."

Then he smiled at Evie. A paternal and loving smile that brought tears to her grieving heart. She would not allow herself to cry in front of him. This whole situation was impossible and unacceptable.

The sun had traveled west on its journey, and Patrick no longer sat basking in its warmth. His face, so recently golden in the warmth of the sunshine, was now pallid and worn.

"Come, child. Help an old man to his bed." Patrick held out his hand and Evie assisted the frail, almost skeletal man across the floor. The sunshine had warmed the wood and she could almost feel the heat rise up as she crossed the stream of rays. She performed a task which the old man had done for her countless times in the years of her childhood. She couldn't bear the thought that soon she would no longer have him around to comfort and advise her.

Coming to see him had just reminded her how close she was to losing him forever.

CHAPTER 4

*D*ejected, Evie left Patrick to rest and headed to her first class of the morning.

The sun was high, spilling warm and bright into the hallways of the Learning Wing. Along the wood-paneled passages, students loitered around, ambled along or rushed headlong toward their classes. Not every Nephilim Warrior cared for learning about the history of mortals. It was uncanny how many Nephilim bore a certain inbred arrogance toward humans despite their role of protectors. But Patrick had insisted they obtain the knowledge in order to better understand the creatures they protected.

Slowly the halls emptied and Evie breathed easier. She disliked crowds and usually avoided the rush, slipping into her classes at the last minute. Next was Ancient Human History. Brother Remus would be introducing Ancient Rome and its first Emperors. Ancient History had always fascinated her, especially anything which predated her own birth year, 1003 AD. Nephilim received longevity, almost immortality, through the blood of their angelic fathers. *Or Angelic mothers,* Evie thought with a wry twist to her lips. The Heavenly Army may just have had a preference for male warriors as Evie had heard of so few female angels in her lifetime.

Although she didn't want to think such blasphemous thoughts, the words "sexist" and "chauvinistic" crawled into her brain. Her eyes darted around before she remembered the Estate was a no-mind-reading-zone as of Marcellus' take-over. She shivered. Not a thing she should forget if she wanted to stay out of trouble.

She grabbed a seat at the back of the class. In spite of her location, Brother Remus would surely throw any number of questions at her. She didn't mind the stares of the other Nephilim as long as they returned their attention to the front of the class and left her alone once she'd given her answers. Most of the Warriors steered clear of Evie, were intimidated by her. By her power, if not by her guardian.

Evie was different. A breed apart from the rest of the Nephilim. Stronger, smarter, more powerful. With the uncomfortable tendency of winning every sparring match and shooting every target, she wasn't the most popular angel on the block. It made for a lonely childhood, spent mostly in the company and friendship of humans. An angel relegated to walk the steps of childhood while watching her friends grow old and wither within the clutches of an inevitable death.

Lately, Evie had begun to question her solitary lifestyle. If Ling and Ash had not joined the Brotherhood, she may have left Patrick's care. She'd had no real friends until the two Nephilim had arrived.

Usually the lesson absorbed all of Evie's attention, but her conversation with Patrick echoed in her ears. She alternated between simmering anger and aching pain, knowing the only father she had ever known was at death's ddoor-somewhere he should never have been. She heard the names Augustus Caesar and Brutus and her head shot up. Just in time too, as Brother

Remus began his usual barrage of questions, sending them randomly at the class.

This time, Evie sat back deflated, as Brother Remus passed her over. She suppressed a sigh. How she would have loved to live in Ancient Rome. Even Patrick had such romantic things to say about that time in history. The thought sobered her, bringing her thudding back to the reality of not having Patrick around to regale her with tales from his long, long ago youth.

Patrick had taken on Evangeline as a favor to a friend. But he had treated the task with immense attention and care, showering Evie with everything from education to friendship to genuine affection. Evie could clearly recall a monastery from her childhood. She was perhaps six years old, and the fragrant scent of thyme and rosemary on a warm summer night still teased her nose. She'd been chasing a butterfly around the courtyard, and followed the shimmering insect right into the air as it rose to escape her fat little fingers. Horrified, Patrick had grabbed hold of her feet, almost choking on his scolds as she strained to fly off on tiny, weak wings, wings which had sprouted from her back without any warning, surprising both herself and especially Patrick. That was the day he fully realized his little charge Evangeline was an angel.

Evie's memories of history from that point on were hazy at best. Patrick had vowed to keep her safe. The vow had translated to being cooped up and hidden away from everything important that had ever happened in the world's history. Evie had missed centuries of important events like the Crusades and the Renaissance. Now she suppressed a sigh. Too many important historical events to dwell on. But Patrick had often said he'd rather give up his mortality than ever allow anything to happen to her, and Evie had conceded that if he were willing to sacrifice that much for her, then she could make him happy by being careful and minding him.

Evie settled into the lesson and tuned everyone and everything out, now focusing her thoughts on a world she'd been born too late to experience. Too soon she would have to face her reality, but for the moment, she enjoyed losing herself in the all-too intangible past.

~

THE HISTORY LESSON passed without a hitch, followed closely by Religion Studies.

At lunch, Evie headed to the Warriors' common room, which doubled as a dining room for the forty-odd Nephilim living on the grounds of Greylock Estate. The last of the morning sun poured through the floor-to-ceiling windows at a steep, slowly-disappearing slant. Evie found her two friends dozing in the lazy sunshine. They'd all had late nights, charging around the Eastern seaboard, eliminating each of their targets on Marcellus' orders. Evie knew exactly how they were feeling, especially since training never stopped in spite of the recent increase in nightly missions.

Ash looked up as Evie clomped to the nest of couches near the open glass doors. A weak breeze floated inside, doing nothing to relieve the blanket of lethargy that lay upon the two girls.

"Hey girl!" Ash grinned and wriggled over to clear some space just in time as Evie plonked herself into the soft cushion and closed her eyes. She tilted her face so she got the full brunt of the sun's warmth while she was still in its path. "What's with the long face, Eves?"

"Humph!" Evie just grunted, not wanting to spoil the luxury of the sun's warm fingers on her skin.

Ash wriggled beside her, enough to force Evie to crack her eyes open a tiny bit to see what she was up to. Ash turned beside her on the couch and wagged an accusing finger at her.

"You've been to see Patrick, haven't you?" Ash pinned Evie with a stare that spoke volumes. Evie just got distracted by her friend's eyes. Glossy, black flecks gleamed deep within green and hazel eyes. Ashika Deva was an Apsara, beautiful and powerful, and super smart. And sometimes super bossy. She continued to glare at Evie, then turned out of her accusatory twist to sit straight-backed on the lumpy couch. Not a position easily maintained when in the throes of lethargy. "Well? That face is gonna sour the milk in my latte, so spill. Now!"

"I don't get it. How does an Immortal die of a mystery illness without someone being able to find out what is going on?" Evangeline's sigh was frustration and desperation all wrapped up in one gigantic shiny layer of suspicion. "Nothing is supposed to be powerful enough to fell an Immortal. He's fading away."

"Should I even bother to ask if Marcellus has called anyone for help?"

"*He* claims he has. He's been required by the council to advise the details of each practitioner who sees Patrick. And maybe there have been a few specialists who have seen him, but really, if Marcellus wants to block the Council from knowing anything, he sure as hell can!" Evie shook her head, anger-filled tears brimming over. "I do know Castor's been to see him for his pains."

"That lunatic? He'll kill poor Patrick faster than whatever illness the poor man has." Ash's eyebrows teased her unruly bangs. Her dark hair was caught at the back of her head, leaving just those bangs to soften the edge of her perfect, oval face, almond eyes fringed heavily with to-die-for lashes would have been the perfect finish were they not filled with an expression of utter disgust. "Why do you let him get near the old guy?"

"Because he'd never harm him. And because I couldn't stop him even if I tried. Castor's been with Patrick all his life." Evie threw Ash a disapproving stare. Ash knew Castor's tale as well as anyone else. But it made no impression on her opinion of his talent as a Healer.

The offspring of a demon and a human, Castor had been cast aside by his horrified mother. Patrick had taken him in, cared for him. Today, he lurked around the estate, acting as healer and shaman to those who dared to call for him, though many of his patients shivered with fear under his ministrations. The poor fellow wasn't unaware of his effect on the general public, so he was always careful to remain hidden within the folds of his hooded garb while he administered his treatment.

Many were given to wonder what sort of demon magic he infused in the salves or oils he used. But Evie never gave it a second thought. She had the utmost trust in Castor because she knew his heart. None knew better than Evie the gratitude the half-demon felt toward Patrick, and the grief the poor Halfling felt for Patrick's impending demise.

"Doesn't change the fact that he creeps me out!" Ash affected a delicate shiver, then fell back into the cushions, all pretense of straight-backed primness gone.

"I'll second that." Evie turned to Ling, whose words were slightly slurred from sleep.

"Snobs are what you two are."

Ling shrugged and Evie sensed the same movement next to her. Li Ling's up-tilted almond eyes shouted her Asian heritage.

"So what's really bothering you? Apart from our distaste in the rabble you associate with?" Ash raised an eyebrow and Evie conceded. She may as well spill her fears to the two girls.

"I just think there's way more to Patrick's illness than just the tail end of his days. And I think he may be questioning his illness too. He probably doesn't want to worry us." Evie bit her lip, hoping she would not regret this confidence. "Don't you find it strange and convenient that Patrick's illness began when Marcellus first approached the Council with his application for the Mastership? Remember how everyone, including Patrick, was so surprised? And then Patrick began to get sick just when it looked like he would oppose Marcellus' bid?"

Both girls stared at Evie, finally comprehending the full extent of Evie's worries.

"But wouldn't you need really powerful magic to kill an Immortal?" Ash scowled, her fine eyebrows scrunched up as she considered the possibility that Evie may be on to something. "Does Marcellus have friends in low places then?"

"That's what is intriguing. Nobody really knows that much about Marcellus. Except that he's been with the Irin for the last ten years. He served Patrick for a decade without any indication he was unhappy. Then he up and usurped the Mastership. And he has Daniel as his uber-eager, right-hand-man."

"Oooh, he's delicious!" Ash sighed as if about to swoon.

Evie jabbed her in the ribs. "Even if he's hot, it doesn't make him any less creepy. And what's with the demands for the metals from the demon kills?"

"Yeah. You weren't the only one who found that odd. What would Marcellus want demon jewelry for?" Ling asked.

"Have you given him everything you've found?" Evie looked at both girls.

"Yeah! What would I need demon stuff for?" It was clear that Ash faced both the demons and the job of dispatching them with equal disgust.

"Hey, easy! Just wanted to check if any of you guys have kept anything back."

"Have you?" Ash probed.

"Er...yes. I have a few things with me. It just seemed so strange that he'd ask such a thing. I can't figure out why he'd need that junk or why he's so desperate to ensure we hand them all over." Evie frowned at Ling, whose eyes were concentrating on the door to the common room and not on the conversation at hand. She was so easily distracted.

Neither of the other girls had an answer for Evie. The sun had passed overhead and no longer shone directly into the room. Evie was beginning to get frustrated with the feeling of helplessness that seemed to permeate the air around the Warriors these days.

The girls struggled out of the couch reluctantly, knowing they had to get going. They had uniforms to change and warm-ups to complete before the afternoon classes. Theoretical and Practical Combat including Chinese Martial Arts for this semester. Followed by Daily Debrief.

"Right then. Back to it!" Ash grabbed the two girls' arms, linked them, and pulled them out of the room. Evie sighed. Perhaps she could just enjoy the afternoon without thinking about doom and gloom and the funny feeling in the pit of her stomach that said something bad was about to happen.

CHAPTER 5

$\mathcal{E}$vie shut her room door behind her and locked it. She'd hidden the strange piece of carved metal behind a lose brick in the fireplace and the last thing she needed was for someone to walk in on her while she took another look at the ring. And she needed to change before the afternoon combat sessions. She was keen to have a look at the disk before she left for class.

She went to the fireplace and ran her hand along the inside of the chimney about two bricks above her shoulder. Where a brick should have sat, was now a hollow, which housed a few of the metal pieces she'd recovered as well as the one special piece that had so caught her eye.

Her fingers closed around the metal disk and Evie slowly removed it. It clinked against the stone mantelpiece and a sweet ringing echoed around the room. Evie clasped the disk close to her chest, glancing at the door and hoping to stop the ringing as she shielded it with her hands and body. Soon the sound died down and the door remained shut. Only then did Evie feel safe enough to inspect the disk. The metal was engraved with eight different designs, each depicting a different scene.

The edges of the disk were about an inch in height and the piece filled Evie's open palm. She stared at the disk a few moments more, seeing nothing more than she had seen before. She sighed and dipped her fingers into the little hidey-hole, depositing the disk back into the relative safety of the brick hideaway.

Evie stepped away from the fireplace and dusted her hands before sitting at the edge of the bed, trying to recall if she'd found anything else with similar markings before. But she came up with nothing. She'd wanted to tell Patrick about the disk, but she'd been terribly afraid to upset him. Patrick was a stickler for the rules and he was sure to blow his top at her for disobeying her Master.

Evie clenched her fist. This subservient role was getting old fast. It may have been easier while Patrick was her Master because she loved him, but she had neither respect nor affection for her new Master, especially not when he treated all the Nephilim like circus animals. To perform as he bid them. Do as he told, no questions asked.

At her bedside sat a small heap of random metal pieces she'd also retrieved from her recent kills. They didn't seem as important as the disk. Perhaps she'd pass them on to Marcellus anyway. She made a note to hide them away, just not with the disk in the fireplace. She cast a forlorn eye over the traitorous rocks and yearned for the days when her work was simple and good.

Combat classes were in a few minutes. And in Debrief, they'd all be getting their next targets. Evie sighed and stared off into space. There must be more to life than killing for Marcellus. Shockingly, Evie found herself considering the possibility of leaving the service of the Irin. But not before she figured out what was going on with Marcellus. And what he had to do with Patrick's illness.

❦

EVIE WAS ZIPPING up her boot, stowing the last of her knives when the door slammed open, crashing so hard against the wall it vibrated as it hit the stone behind it. Evie was sure the brass knob had left a nice enough dent in the wall. She didn't have much time to wonder how the door had opened when she'd been so careful to ensure it was locked tight. The room was suddenly filled with a dozen of Marcellus' new army of bodyguards.

"What's going on? What are you doing coming in here?" Evie was not overly modest having been around for so many centuries, but she was still young at heart. Had they stormed in just five minutes earlier she would have been very much undressed, and very much pissed off. Right now, she was pretty pissed anyway. "This room is private and off limits."

She rose to her feet, pulling herself up to her full height. All Nephilim were tall, but she towered over most of the men. Being six foot, she was often taller than most mortals. The group of men held their stance in the face of Evie's height and her boiling anger. Seemed they were not afraid of little old Evie. Perhaps they were misled by her youthful, gamine facade? Evie shivered with anger, slowly losing the battle to contain her fury. Her shoulders pulsated, her bones shifted beneath the skin of her back, and her neck grew heavy. In the next instant, her wings exploded behind her in a rush of white and silver feathers.

The sudden appearance of her wings did two things. The mini-whirlwind it created startled the band of armed men encircling her. It also instilled the leaden weight of fear in her attackers. The circle around Evie widened as each of the men took a step backward, alarm etched on each separate face.

A hiss of impatience and annoyance announced the presence of Marcellus somewhere behind the black rank of bodyguards. The very existence of this small army of guards had raised the ire of many members of the Brotherhood. Patrick had overseen the Irin for over a millennia and never did he feel the need to protect his back. Never felt threatened in any way. Perhaps it was true; it was the guilty who feel the need for protection. Marcellus sure had something to hide.

"Fools!" He shouldered the men aside and placed himself nose-to-chest in front of Evie. For a man whose intention was to rule the ancient Brotherhood of Irin with the hand of fear, he was incongruously diminutive. Despite his lack of stature, he resonated an essence of negative energy. Energy which Evie sensed was black and filled with hate and anger. Evie wanted to step away from him. She felt violated just by sharing personal space with the man.

But stepping away would acknowledge his authority and confirm her status as a mere servant. Evie was getting tired of her servitude. She stared him down. And he was the first to turn away. He glared hotly at his men. "She won't hurt you, you idiots."

Now where did he get that idea from? Why would he be so confident that I wouldn't harm him or his men?

He turned to Evie. His eyes grazed her from the tips of her shiny boots, to the silvery glow on the edges of her wings as they undulated behind her. His gaze remained on her wings a few seconds more, before he dismissed them.

"Impressive. But so unnecessary." His eyes were cold, flat. None of the usual admiration or respect which Evie was so used to whenever she stood shadowed by the glory of her angelic nature.

It was possible he wanted her to retract her wings, but with Marcellus, every action had a meaning. And retraction would be tantamount to an admission that he was not only Master of the Irin but Master of Evangeline too. And Evie would die before she fell at his feet.

"What do you want?" Evie asked softy.

"I do believe you have been holding something from me?" Marcellus' eyes pierced her, a hawk watching for the slightest twitch.

Evie brows knitted in confusion. "Huh?"

He walked around Evie, keeping his distance from the shimmering tips of the feathers behind her. "I have it on good authority that you have been stealing from me?"

"Stealing? That's the most ridiculous thing I've ever heard." By now Evie's head was hot, her blood simmering with rage at Marcellus' invasion of her privacy and now his accusation.

He made a circling motion above his head and commanded, "Search the room. Bring me what you find."

The men fanned out and began searching. A lamp crashed to the ground and Marcellus winced before he could restrain himself. Evie looked straight at him, hot anger still flaring in her eyes. "Anything that is damaged or broken—you will replace. This is my home! And that was a Ming Dynasty authentic piece."

"Try not to break anything, boys." Marcellus remained in front of Evie's face and crossed his arms while an expression of amusement washed his deep features. The skin on his face was a pasty white, his hair stringy and balding, and the muscles beneath the fabric of his cloak soft and puny. A lot can be said for stature, but Napoleon had long managed to make everyone around him forget that he was often the shortest person in the room. It had to do with personality. And Marcellus' personality seemed to want to pull him down. Probably down to where he belonged—within the fiery depths of the Underworld. Hades, Hell, Patala, he simply had to chose which one.

A grunt from one of his men and a rush of boot heels on the wood floor—they had discovered the pile of metal she'd scavenged from her last few kills. Evie remained unmoved. His man dropped the collection into Marcellus' open palm. He rifled through them, nonchalant. As if he knew that what he searched for was not there. Immediately Evie thought about the disk. He was after the disk, but there was no way he'd have known she'd anything specific in her possession.

"Are there any more?"

She shook her head, her eyes narrowing dangerously. After all the years living with humanity Evie had learned well the art of deceit.

"Hopefully you will remember this. Ensure you bring me every piece of metal you find."

He drew so close his face was a mere inch away from hers. She squelched the urged to laugh. She knew he must have raised himself at least to the balls of his feet to get this close. The idea was so comical that his attempt at intimidation fell far short. "Every piece of metal. Do you understand? It is vital. Not only to me, but to the existence of the Irin itself."

I wonder what that means? Evie thought as she smelled the noxious remnants of Marcellus' lunch on his breath. Stale garlic and weak tea. Awful. She forced herself to stop her nose from wrinkling in his face. But she needn't have bothered.

He was already turning on his heel and walking out the door. But then he paused abruptly, looking back at Evie with a hand on the doorjamb. "I know you will follow the rules, Evangeline. If not for your loyalty to me, then for your fealty to the old and ailing Master, Patrick."

That sneering smile stayed with Evie for hours after. The subtle threat stayed longer.

THE TEAM usually met in the common room before the afternoon classes. This day was no different, except each of the girls had similar expressions of shock plastered on pale faces. Other Warriors milled around also waiting for the next class. The girls moved to an unoccupied end of the long dining table.

"They got to you too?" Ash asked Evie as she sat down and dragged her chair closer. Eating was the last thing on her mind. Mainly because her mind was too busy processing her suspicions. Suspicions of what Marcellus wanted with the metal pieces. Suspicions of how he'd known she'd kept back some of the metal pieces. Suspicions of who would have told.

"Yeah. They came crashing into my room and took whatever I hadn't handed to Marcellus during this past week." Evie's eyes narrowed as she studied the two other girls. Both looked equally shaken, but it could have been either one of them who had ratted her out. They were the only two people she had confided in. "It brings me to the question of how Marcellus had known I still had the pieces with me."

Knowing she still had the disk tucked away in the fireplace hideout, Evie wasn't terribly angry about losing the other random junk. It was really the knowledge that she had been betrayed that stuck in her gut.

"If you're trying to accuse us of something, Miss E, come right out and say it, okay?" Ash flashed her baby greens at Evie, tapping her foot while she waited for a response.

"I'm not accusing anyone. I don't want to accuse anyone of anything. But I told only the two of you. Who else could have known about it?"

"Kara knew too," Ling announced. "She came in while we were talking. Then she turned fast and went back out. But since she left, I thought that was that. Then she grabbed me in the corridor on the way to my room. She asked if we were also keeping stuff from Marcellus and confided she was too."

Evie shook her head slowly, her lip twisting, the action both reproachful and regretful. Ling lifted her shoulders sadly. "C'mon, Evie, it's not my fault!"

Evie, deep in thought, patted Ling's arm distractedly and said, "It doesn't matter, Ling. If Kara ratted us out, we'll just have to find out why."

Evie wondered what Kara's reason would be to betray the team. Ling awkwardly embraced a worried Evie and said, "Don't stress, sister. I have a surprise for you."

Evie raised her eyebrows at Ling and said a silent, thankful prayer for the presence of these two girls. Living a long life was only worthwhile if you had decent companions.

Ling drew an object from her satchel and handed it to Evie. Wrapped in a soft scarf, the weight of the package felt decidedly familiar.

"No, don't peek. Let's take it somewhere private before you let everyone see it. It's going to be a secret!" Ling grinned.

CHAPTER 6

*B*ack in Ling's room, which was closest to the common hall, the girls huddled on the bed and studied the disk which had been hidden within the folds of one of Ling's Pashminas. Only Heaven knew when Ling got the chance to wear things like scarves and gloves, but the girl loved them. Evie would rather have a new sword, and she knew Ash was eyeing a new set of those spinning spears she loved.

Evie's fingers traced the markings and symbols on the disk. It was identical to the one hidden in her chimney except for one symbol which was more heavily outlined on this particular disk. It's possible that each disk had a particular meaning or signified one particular symbol on the disk. It would so help to know what the symbols meant, though.

"Wow! That's beautiful. How come I wasn't lucky enough to find one of these?" Ash sighed dramatically.

"So, what do you reckon I should do? Hand it over to Short-stuff before he attacks me for it?" asked Ling. Ash giggled.

The memory of Marcellus on tippy-toes coming nose to nose with Evie earlier sent her into her own spasm of giggles. It didn't take long for her to sober up, though.

As much as Evie wanted to offer to keep it with her, she wanted to ensure the girls had no reason to see her as anything but neutral regarding the disks. "I'd say hold onto it unless it's going to endanger you. We still need to figure out how Marcellus found out about us holding back in the first place. Did either of you have anything like this taken away?"

Both girls said no. "I had this in the armory," Ling offered.

"Well, put it back then, and let's find out what the deal is with Kara."

The girls left Ling's room, hurrying first to the armory and then to their combat class.

MASTER MARCELLUS LOVED to hold court. His daily briefings were held in the largest conference room, which overlooked the entire front garden of the estate. Each of the senior Warriors were seated around a conference table purported to be the largest on the eastern seaboard, carved from a single piece of ancient white oak. As magnificent as the table was, it couldn't hold a candle to the immense crystal chandelier that lit its meticulously polished surface.

Someone should have to told Shortstuff that all this opulence will take some of the attention off of him, Evie thought. She was not in a magnanimous mood, especially not since the privacy of her room was in serious question. Both Ash and Ling were equally unimpressed.

Patrick had always held his debriefs in his library at the end of the day with all the members gathered around him in a comfortable circle. He knew how to claim and keep the attention and the passion of the Nephilim who served the Irin. A motley crew, they had shared the desire to assist Patrick in his mission to help those in need. But now, that passion was waning. Marcellus ran the ship with a tight fist, and their love for the job was quickly fading.

Evie had to force herself to pay attention. Daniel began to hand out folders to each member, puffed with his own importance. Done, he took up position at his Master's right hand, awaiting his next instruction. His subservient demeanor downplayed the hard intelligence that shone from his eyes when he thought nobody was watching. Evie didn't trust him for a second.

Marcellus' voice broke through her thoughts. "Each of you now have your instructions and your targets. Any questions?"

No responses from the table.

"I am sure most of you need not be reminded, again, of my request regarding anything of a metal construct found on any of your marks. It is imperative that each and every item be returned to me immediately upon your return to base." Marcellus turned his head and looked straight at Evie. "There may be those among you who will question that instruction, but let me remind you of this. You serve the Brotherhood. Not the other way around."

He panned the room with those clear grey eyes.

Evie felt a wave of dissatisfaction ripple around the table. Marcellus' words were not going down well with the three teams present. Whether he knew it or not, the Grand Master of the Irin had just sown the seeds of rebellion, however miniscule.

FILING out of the room with the rest of the team, Evie gripped the paper folder tightly. She was both keen on knowing who Marcellus needed her to kill, and looking forward to learning more about what he was up to. Perhaps a little demon interrogation might do the trick. But it still angered her that she worked for that madman.

A voice beside her pulled her out of her thoughts. "What the hell was that all about?" Flash asked, his eyes matching his name. "That sucker's going from bad to worse."

Evie was uncertain how to handle Flash's question. She had so many questions about Marcellus' intentions that she was beginning to be overly suspicious. To see spies in every friend and traitors around every corner.

"Not sure, Flash. It seem pretty weird, this new take on our missions."

"Yeah. Not sure how much more of this I can take." Flash's face was etched with fatigue, his eyes lined with red veins.

"What you been up to? You look trashed." She frowned, studying his face a little closer.

"Huh? Oh...Algeria today, the Pyrenees tomorrow, and the Sahara yesterday." His shoulders slumped. "Enough to make a man cry."

Flash was another Nephilim whose strength and power was unquestioned within the Brotherhood. Clearly why they worked him so hard.

"You really should slow down. You don't want to have those fabulous wings jam on you while you're thirty miles up in the sky."

Flash smiled and shook his head, regret clear in his eyes. "Not much of a chance, girl. While I'm here, and while Shortstuff keeps on this metal foraging tack of his, there will be no rest for any of us. Especially not the ones he has already collared like dogs."

"What's that supposed to mean?"

"Who do you think ratted you out?" Flash stared at Evie, forcing her to question herself. "Even if you don't want to know, its Kara. He's had her under his thumb for a while now. You might want to have a chat with her before she gets you in trouble big time."

With a wink he tipped her a tiny salute and shuffled down the hall with the rest of the teams. Ash and Ling had given her some space while she and Flash were talking and were waiting just ahead. Ash raised her eyebrows and produced a silent wolf whistle. Ling just rolled her eyes and pulled her along down the hall. So Flash was a hottie. Evie wasn't interested.

"You two make a smokin' couple." Ash smiled with a distinct matchmaker gleam.

"Not interested," Evie answered, her thoughts still on Flash. Why would he give her Kara? Was he helping her or was he just getting her on a different track away from the real traitor—himself?

"You're kidding, right? You keep playing hard to get, he's gonna take his Flash and sizzle elsewhere."

"Ash, I keep telling you, he's not interested in me that way. And even if he was, I certainly am not. I don't have the time for a relationship. Besides, I have plenty of years ahead of me to dedicate to a love life."

"Yeah, we know, your first priority is to find good old Gabe." Ash shook her head. "I feel sorry for you.... You do know you are probably chasing a ghost, right?"

"I will find him."

"Yeah... and you'll be looking for him for another few centuries before the trail starts getting warm."

Evie nodded and met Ling's eyes. Ling raised an eyebrow in question and looked at her hand. Evie took note of the set of three thin acupuncture needles the other girl rolled between her forefinger and thumb. Ling would have at least seven ways to use those needles to incapacitate an opponent. And she wasn't against using it on Ash, especially when she got into one of her random lectures. Evie laughed and shook her head.

Ash, distracted by the sound, looked from Ling to Evie and then to Ling's hand. She fell into a fit of tickled laughter. "Don't you even think about it, Ling! Gosh you two. I'm gonna have to keep one eye open when I sleep."

"Only if you continue your little matchmaking plot." Evie waggled a warning finger at the still-giggling Ash.

"Hhmmm! I'm so afraid." Ash turned around and walked down the passage, knocking her knees together as she went. She looked ridiculous. Evie and Ling fell into step behind her and laughed all the way to dinner.

AFTER THE EVENING MEAL, the girls parted ways to prepare for the night's work. As of yet, Evie had not admitted to anyone on her team that she was in possession of one of the mysterious disks. She had been tempted to ask Ling to hand her disk over so she could hide it with its partner. But Ling was a possessive creature, and until Evie found out more about the true purpose of these disks, it would be best not to cause further friction within the team. Evie had gone looking for Kara, hoping to have a little chat with the other Nephilim, but oddly she'd been unable to find her. And strangely enough, Marcellus had not remarked on her absence, sent out a search party, or shown any concern about her unexplained absence from the grounds.

Evie's file had informed her that she'd been assigned to a demon in the Bayou. She wrinkled her nose. She hated swamps, mosquitoes, and humidity. And tramping around in the thick of all three did not sound like fun. She supposed she could stop for beignets on the way back. Make herself feel a tiny bit better.

The paper crinkled in her hand and Evie scanned the printout.

Demon, second class. Name: Renfru. The printed sheet contained information as to his exact whereabouts and nothing else.

Evie sighed. This was not good enough. These new orders were nothing like Patrick's missions. He'd sent them on aid missions. Not that they never had the odd assassination to perform, but they were first and foremost protectors of the people. Since Marcellus took over, the Warriors had become glorified killers, assassins, and Evie wanted it stopped.

Her first port of call would be Patrick. He'd most likely be less inclined to advise her in any action against the new order, but at least he would be able to give her an opinion on the disks themselves.

HER KNOCK at Patrick's door was firm and loud. She hoped he'd hear her as she entered. Her eyes went straight for the bed and Evie's heart and hopes plunged. Patrick lay upon the white pillows, pale, and wrinkled and grayed. Corpselike. The thought sent Evie flying to his side. She gasped as she gripped his hand and still felt warmth, then berated herself for fearing the worst. She'd expected the icy cold fingers of death.

Patrick's eyes cracked open and she felt her heartbeat slowly return to normal. She hesitated, guilt stabbing through her as she gazed at his frail form. He barely had the strength to open his eyes and here she was so ready to burden him with her worries.

"I'm still here, Evangeline. No need to fret." Even his smile was weak and frail.

She snorted. "Fret? Whatever makes you think I'd fret for you, old man?" She squeezed his hand and sent up a plethora of prayers.

"What's the matter, child? I can feel the negative energy rolling off you," he asked as he moved himself upward to lean against the pillows piled against the headboard.

Evie sat beside him on the bed. "I promised I wouldn't bother you with these concerns, but it's gotten so much worse today." She paused, unsure where to begin. "I asked you earlier about metal on the demons and what the Brotherhood may want with them."

Patrick nodded.

"Well then, what would Marcellus want with this?" As she posed the question, Evie drew the disk from her pocket. She turned the old man's hand over and laid the metal in the middle of his weathered palm.

Patrick was silent as he stared at the disk. It was solid metal. Heavy. He lifted the ring to his eyes and studied it closely. He looked quite strange, squinting at the piece from various angles. He'd seemed to have drawn energy from somewhere because he was suddenly lively enough to ask for his pencil and paper. He lay the paper over the disk, then using the pencil, ran the edge over the ridges of the engravings, working slowly, meticulously, taking a copy of it. Somehow, the symbols appeared clearer on the penciled copy.

"And?" Evie prodded.

"And nothing," Patrick answered, his voice breaking harshly on the words. He paused to clear his throat. "I'm afraid I cannot help you. It's fascinating and beautiful. But I haven't the faintest idea of its origin or its purpose." He shrugged and laid the disk back into Evie's hand, closing her fingers over the warmed metal. For one fleeting second, she thought she saw his forehead scrunch with worry and fear.

When she looked again his expression was clear and impassive. "It certainly doesn't look like much, but I'd take good care of it if I were you."

Patrick's manner seemed unperturbed, and he fell into a solemn silence, looking off into the shadows of the far corner of the room.

"Patrick," Evie called him softly, but she already knew he was off somewhere in his head, in that place he went where everything probably felt easier to deal with. She couldn't possibly begrudge him that. With a small sigh, she rose and left him there alone with his thoughts.

At the door she took one last glance at the old man and left feeling unsettled but more sure than ever that Patrick knew more than he was telling.

The disks were important and Patrick wasn't willing to help.

CHAPTER 7

*B*ecause of Marcellus, Evie was now flying the thirteen hundred miles to New Orleans. At this height, all she could see of the millions of little lives far, far below her were constant, glimmering specks of light. The air was cool on her cheeks as she flew. Her wings were strong, muscles corded, energy flowing through bones and flesh until the heat of it reached the very tips of her feathers. It still amazed her, the power and strength of those twin appendages of flight.

They allowed her to rise above humanity in a way that satisfied her deepest need. The need to distance herself from the sameness, the platitudes, the non-individuality of humans. Sure, human blood swam through her veins at this minute, but it seemed to Evie that her angelic blood often warred with and won over the lowly human DNA. She had certainly never consciously chosen a side; her angelic side seemed to win that internal tug-of-war all by itself. Until she'd learned more about humanity and seen the destruction they wrought on their own flesh and blood.

Now as she flew, Evie succumbed to the peace and serenity of the darkness. The moon was a shameful sliver hanging low in the sky. Not enough light to reveal the Nephilim as she headed to the

Mississippi bayou that hid her next mark. Even so, Evie always flew with a glamor, guarding her presence from inadvertent observation. The skies had grown busier in the last century, and she never knew when she'd come across a low-flying plane or be spotted by a satellite.

Somewhere ahead, New Orleans lay on the horizon, hidden beneath the clouds, steeped in muggy, tepid air. Evie was here for Renfru—a particular demon in a prominent position in the hierarchy of Earth-side Demonica. Renfru. Just a name. Demons were blessed, no surname. Not that they would fit right into human society with such singular titles. Like all aliens living within the borders of the US, demons were forced to make the effort to obtain the necessary paperwork. From social security numbers and driver's licenses to credit cards and passports, they had everything covered to live the ordinary American life.

Their only problem was if you knew how to look, you'd find them. Evie sniggered. She had the luxury only because she could see right through a demon's glamor, while her own Heaven-powered glamor was impenetrable even to a high-level demon. She could stand right next to one of the brutes without the slightest danger of being discovered. Again she revered her angelic nature.

The Big Easy drew closer, reminding Evie of her mark's address. She hated swamps with a passion. Not that she was unable to stay dry. It was just the odor of wet sand and standing water, and the presence of so many alligators lurking below the deceptively calm waters. Evie didn't fear an alligator bite. But the possibility of being snapped at by rows of vicious teeth gave her the heebie-jeebies.

Now above the swamps, she flew lower, hovering over the lonely, darkened wetlands. Somewhere within its murky depths lay the home of the next demon she was required to dispatch. She felt the now familiar jab of her conscience, daring her to question if what she was doing was the right thing. How much longer could she go on doing Marcellus' bidding?

Evie pushed the thought out of her head and tried to concentrate on her assigned task. She just had the coordinates to work with, but they were enough. Her internal GPS tracking was faultless. Evie flew lower; the hushed whir of her wings doused her with longing. This was the only time she had to herself. The only time not under Marcellus' control.

As she dropped gently from the sky, a fine layer of moisture bathed her heated skin. The evening still bore the remnants of a hot and sticky day, and even the atmosphere was unable to summon cool and refreshing condensation.

Evie smiled. If Ash were here, she'd be fretting that the high humidity would destroy that pin-straight style she'd adopted recently. She passed over the city, her ears teased by the strains of grumbling cars and tooting horns. She headed a few miles out to Bayou Sauvage. The weak light of the moon threw the barest layer of gray illumination on the cypress swamp.

Evie hovered over the skulking river, which travelled so slowly an observer could be excused for assuming it was just a pool of standing water. The surface was littered with moldy leaves, while jerky rustling hinted at the presence of a frog or two. The closer she drew, the more distinct the sound of the bayou night became. Cicadas and frogs threw a symphony of chirps and croaks across the darkened waters. She took a deep breath and tasted musty air.

Along one of those incredibly tired tributaries, sat a dilapidated wooden house. Such a poor excuse for a home. It would better answer to the name of shack. Evie lowered herself over the building and landed on the aluminum roof with a grimace of distaste. She kept her glamor tightly woven around her as she tested the roof's ability to hold her weight. For all its ramshackle appearance, it was soundly built and the roof held strong beneath her. Evie tensed and retracted her wings, the flutter of it sending her hair into her eyes. She brushed it aside and dropped to her knees, hoping her keen ears would reveal any occupants.

Nothing.

Just the frogs and cicadas competing for attention.

Evie leaped to the ground, landing softly on the balls of her feet. Without her wings she was unable to fly, but short drops were easy as she still retained an essence of anti-gravity. She didn't float, just dropped at a slower rate, allowing her to find her footing more easily. At the entrance of the shack, Evie surveyed the warped wood of the porch that sat lopsided at the front like a dislocated jaw.

A sound traveled to Evie's wary ears. The splash of water. Regular, like a paddle breaking the surface of the river, a gentle waterfall of droplets, and then a slight plunk, only to repeat itself over and over again. The direction from which the sound originated was distorted, unclear as the dense air played with it before delivering it to Evie's ears. Evie sighed and sought cover despite her glamor. The moon had slipped behind a bank of clouds as black as the sky itself. It was now as dark as pitch. She'd have to wait for the intruder to arrive rather than have him plough straight into her in the pitch darkness. She could see clearly enough, but she'd rather not get caught unawares.

The splashing stopped and silence lay upon the bayou, dense and thick as the muggy air. Evie waited, wishing she'd had company. Since Marcellus had taken charge, all the old procedures had flown out of the window. No longer did any of the Nephilim go out in pairs. Their jobs had become lonely, and far more lethal than she was comfortable with. Evie's last few kills had left her feeling confused and worried.

Bushes rustled and moved aside as a dark figure entered the clearing in front of the shack. The figure strode forward, something large and heavy slung over one shoulder weighing him down slightly, injecting a slight roll in his gait. Evie watched him walk to the door, and shove it open with his free shoulder. She followed, careful not to make a sound. She stood at the open door and watched as he dumped the contents of the black bag onto a table that looked like it had seen better days—probably about a century ago. Evie peered around his arm, wanting to reassure herself that the contents of the bag was not some recently deceased wino providing Renfru with his main course for dinner. She was relieved when all she saw was groceries.

He turned to the door then, as if he'd sensed her presence. His eyes searching the porch and the dark night beyond. Seeing nothing, he returned to his task.

Now, Evie studied the man. Demon really, but he looked like a man. A glimmer of sorts sheathed his body as if he wore a clear plastic coating. Like a bubble of water, light refracted against its surface and all the colors of the rainbow glowed around him. *Rather pretty if you didn't remind yourself that he was a demon who hailed from the fiery bowels of Hell.* Evie concentrated and slipped past the shimmer of his glamor, to the real Renfru. She shivered a little. *Boy was he ugly.* Well, she'd have to consider this another practical lesson in demon appearance. Evie was hoping to avoid the dissection part of the lesson.

Renfru's outer appearance was human and attractive. In reality, he had deep red skin the same shade as the blood in Evie's veins. His own blood, like all demons, was black, like oil, thick and slick. Deep grooves patterned Renfru's face, as if he'd been cut and scarred some time in his youth. Evie and the rest of her classmates were equally surprised to find that demons had similar childhoods and growth patterns to all the races of Nephilim. Patrick had called them the Black Ones, meaning the Black Nephilim. Ash and Ling were not impressed at being cate- gorized with demons, but were they not all children of the angels anyway? The thought made Evie want to shudder but she controlled the urge and focused on the mark.

A cupboard door slammed inside a dark corner of the shack. Renfru turned and walked straight at Evie. She spun around just in time to avoid being body-slammed by the marching demon. He headed outside, moving to the left of the house. A pile of firewood sat next to a fat log. A gleaming axe leaned against the log. Renfru returned seconds later with an armful of firewood. Before he could take a step toward the house, Evie pounced.

A roundhouse kick to his torso had him lying flat on his back, surprise and fear clear on both his human and un-glamored faces. Firewood went flying in a dozen directions. In a smooth move, Evie grabbed the axe from beside the log and sped to Renfru before he could take one step away. She held it at his throat, at the same time slowly removing her glamor. Renfru's face tightened, surprised and shocked at seeing first a magically flying axe and then a girl appearing right in front of his face.

"Don't move. Don't even blink," Evie whispered, her face an inch from his. "It's your lucky day, Ren. All I want to do is to talk."

Renfru blinked at her in spite of Evie's instruction. She refrained from killing him for his error and listened to his thoughts. They came to her in erratic bursts. *Who is she? What does she want with me? Is it about the groceries?'*

Evie shook her head. "Get up and get inside." She moved off him and allowed him to rise and walk toward the house, all the while holding the blade to his neck. And she was not surprised when he charged away, despite the viciously sharp blade at his neck. She heard the thought before he moved- *Stupid bitch. I'll show her-'*. Typical male, no matter the species. Always had something to prove. Especially when it came to being beat by a girl.

Evie thrust upward on a surge of wings, flapping fast to avoid the sweep of the demon's blade-edged fingers. Stupid, she'd been so focused on Marcellus and his motives, she'd forgotten Renfru was a Ciaptus demon, whose fingers and toes were edged with razor-sharp blades, sufficient for self-defense and much easier to carry around than a sword or a pistol. The human glamor he'd used to cover his real demon self also hid those deadly fingers and equally deadly bare feet.

Any slower and Evie would have had a neat set of five thin, deep cuts on both her legs. Now, just out of reach above Renfru, she was getting impatient.

Renfru, on the other hand, stood, ten fingers raised in the air, as if deep within a strange trance, staring at her as she hovered above him. She heard him draw in a shocked breath, heard him say *'Shit, she's a fucking angel'*. Evie drew her blade from its sheath at her side and threw it. The blade shimmered through the air and landed on target, on the ground right between the demon's legs. She lowered herself down in front of him, confident he knew any attempt to attack her would not be easy.

"We can do this the easy way, or the hard way. Your choice." As she spoke, her wings retracted and disappeared behind her.

"Fine. What do you want?" he answered petulantly, though his eyes flashed and his thoughts were more in line with running for his life.

Evie was happy to remain outside in spite of the moisture-laden air. The night was peaceful with only the cicadas and frogs for company. Somewhere nearby, the low snore of an alligator's bellow drifted to the pair who faced each other in the centre of the clearing.

"Today you get a second lease on life, pal. Do you have anything metal on you?"

"Huh?"

"Look, I don't have time to play games. You need to listen closely—do you have any metal on you?" Evie repeated the words, slowly enunciating each syllable.

"Yeah, course I do."

"Hand it over."

Renfru looked about to utter another "Huh" then thought better of it. He pulled a cord from his neck on which hung a strangely entwined snake which he flung in Evie's direction. Then he dragged his belt from the loops of his pants and threw it at her feet. Two heavy lead rings followed. All items were glamored and had lain on the real Renfru, invisible to any inquisitive eye. Anyone watching him now would think the sudden appearance of these items was some sort of magic trick.

"Is that it?" Evie asked. Renfru hesitated. His eyes flicked to the stump of wood where she'd found the axe, his thoughts about something hidden and his hopes she wouldn't find it. Something he'd hidden in plain sight perhaps? "What else?"

The demon shook his head. "Nothing else." He folded his arms, bulky muscles tightening as if that would convince her to believe him. Evie gave him one last disgusted glance and walked to the stump. She circled it for a moment, studying the footprints around it, the worn patches of grass and the smoothness of the sand in places where it had no business being so smooth.

Then she walked over to the stump, placed her palms on one worn edge and pushed it over. She'd seen the alarm on his face when she'd studied it. Now, her instinct had paid off. Peering inside, she saw a package, wrapped in black cloth and placed in a hollow beneath the twining roots of the stump. She squatted beside the hollow and retrieving it, looking over at the now stricken demon.

He moved his weight from one foot to the other as if contemplating running away again. His eyes flicked from the wrapped object within her hands to her face and back again, sweat beginning to bead his forehead. But she couldn't get a hold of any coherent thoughts. Seemed he was too terrified to think.

Evie rose and walked back to Renfru. She eyed his face, now pinched with his mouth turned down at the corners. He looked like he was about to toss his cookies. Whatever this little package was, so safely hidden in the tree stump, must be quite important. The loss of his jewelry and belt certainly hadn't upset him this much.

Evie weighed the object in her palm, and the familiarity of it made her stomach tighten. It weighed almost the same as the disk hidden in her fireplace back in Greylock. Just the thought made

Evie grab the cloth and throw the folds of fabric open as fast as she could. At last she paused and drew in a breath at what lay tucked within the dark silk.

Inside lay a twin of the disk she had hidden in her room. The same as the one Ling had tucked away in the armory. Evie's heart clenched. This had to mean something. And in that moment she made a decision and prayed that what she intended to do would not be revealed to Marcellus.

Renfru scraped his foot on the sandy ground, bringing Evie back to the present. She noted the sick cast to Renfru's face as his eyes flitted between the disk and her face.

"What is this?" she asked, keeping an eye on his face, his expression.

"Nothing important." He turned his eyes away from Evie's face.

"You expect me to believe that? When the look in your eyes tells me you're so sick with fear you might just throw up? What are you so afraid of?"

"You have no idea what you're dealing with." Renfru's eyes shrunk with fear. They were set too close together anyway, and he ended up looking like a bright red meerkat.

"Then why not tell me?" She stared at him, determined to get her answer. His shoulders bowed and she sensed him losing a little of his fight.

"I can't. I don't have clearance." He wrung his hands together and paced a small spot. He was either plotting his escape or worrying about his fast-approaching death at the hands of his boss.

"Clearance? I take it this trinket is pretty important Down Under?" Evie pointed to the ground.

He didn't reply. Didn't seem to find it very funny.

"Look, I was sent here to kill you. Do you understand that? That'd mean going back home, you know?" From what Evie had learned, most Earth-side Demons got the taste for living the

Upside life and given the chance to return home, would run screaming to the nearest hills.

"Do what you have to." He shrugged, but Evie was not convinced of his nonchalance, especially when his thoughts were fearful: *'If you take that Seal, I'm dead anyway'*

"Seal? Is that what it's called?" Renfru's face filled with shock. He'd be wondering how she knew. But she didn't have time to waste. "Seal for what?"

"Look, just kill me, okay? Better to die now than to wait for the boss to find out I let the Seal slip through my fingers."

"What is this Seal for? What does it do?" Evie closed the distance between them. "Listen, Ren, someone wants these Seals badly enough to kill for it. That means you and all your demon buddies are in permanent danger until this guy finds all the Seals. So I could do with some help here."

"Check with Baltazar. He has the authority to talk if he feels it's necessary."

Evie's heart sank to her stomach on hearing Baltazar's name. She'd taken the Seal he'd had in his possession after she'd sent him back down to his maker. Seemed she'd just killed a potentially vital source.

"Baltazar's dead," she said flatly.

"What? How do I know you aren't lying... to get me to talk?"

"Because I was the one who killed him. Yesterday." Guilt flooded her veins. Her instinct may have been right. Baltazar may not have been the right demon to terminate.

"You killed Baltazar?" Disbelief fractured his glamor and now, the demon stood before her in all his gory glory. Looking as if he'd just lost his best friend.

"Yes. He was my last target." Evie shrugged, trying to pretend it wasn't a big deal.

'And I'm your next.' Renfru's eyes were round with fear.

"That was before I found out there was something strange about these Seals."

Ren's fear was palpable but he must have considered her words meant she wasn't going to kill him just yet. "You have Baltazar's Seal?" When Evie nodded, Renfru asked, "How many do you have already?"

"Does it matter?"

"Of course, it matters! What do you think you are playing with?" Renfru stared at Evie, outraged.

"I don't know. That's why I'm asking you," she said patiently.

"I can't tell you. And now that you've killed Baltazar, you're gonna have to speak to someone higher up than him." Renfru shook his head, his shoulders rounded as if bearing the weight of the world upon them. Evie raised her eyebrows to urge him on. "The only problem is the next guy up is the Boss."

"How is that a problem?" Evie raised an eyebrow, staring the demon down.

"Because he doesn't take uninvited guests lightly," he said. *'Though in your case he might think twice before he kills you.'* Renfru thought and managed a sneer.

Evie smiled and said, "Trust me, I can handle him. I don't want trouble. All I need is information."

"Fine. It's your head." Renfru smiled. Rows of yellow teeth peeked at Evie, pushing the demon higher up on what Ash would call "the ick list."

"Look for Baa'ruk in the French Quarter."

"Does he use his demon name then?" Renfru may have been trying to get her on the wrong track but she was paying attention.

"Goes by the name of Lacroix, Barry Lacroix." Evie smiled at the play on the demon chieftain's real name.

"Thanks." She turned to leave. Over her shoulder she said, "Oh, and you might want to move."

"Why?" Renfru stepped toward her, hands in the air, indignant. Evie wished she could say it was a joke.

"I was sent here to terminate you. I'm going to have to tell my boss you were gone when I got here. And when he does find out you're still alive, he'll send others to check and to complete the job. So for both your and my sake, you'd better clear out."

Evie left with the music of Renfru's curses, both demon and English, trailing after her.

CHAPTER 8

Evie followed Renfru's information on his Boss's nighttime haunts. Her own sense of smell would confirm his presence anyway, but it helped that she had a general starting point. Lafayette Square was dark, lit only by a few hesitant streetlamps along the main pathway. It didn't take long to pick up his scent. Higher-level demons had a stronger, viler odor than their lackeys.

Evie also knew that scent meant power. He would not be an easy mark, so she followed with care, keeping an eye out on the path before her. The oaks dotting the park whispered at her as she passed. Perhaps there were secrets they wished to reveal, but Evie was not faery to understand the trees, so she left them to their whispering and walked on.

Lacroix's scent led her through the trees until the statue of Henry Clay loomed above her. In the darkness, Henry was just a huge metal blob. In the shadow of the towering tribute, Evie paused, searching the gloom. Just before she reached St. Charles Avenue, she saw a flash of white, ghostlike in the edgy shadows. The specter turned and led Evie down the street. Soon the sounds of laughter and nightlife filtered onto the street and Evie found herself entering the French Quarter.

By now she'd gotten a good look at her target. His human glamor was that of a blond, dreadlocked albino. And when Evie strained to look past that milky outside, she found herself surprised. Baa'ruk must have had a deep respect for his melanin-challenged condition, especially since his demon self was equally as blond as his human persona.

Evie absorbed this experience as calmly as she could. A visit with an albino demon would be the hottest discussion topic in their Demonology class. But, right now she felt like a lamb trotting to the slaughter as Baa'ruk strode ahead, forcing her to follow him along Bourbon Street, then down a darkened alley.

CHAPTER 9

*E*vie followed the trail which Baa'ruk laid for her. Head of the Earth-side demons for the Southern Zone meant he would have to be one wily fellow. And seeing as she hadn't had the forethought to request an audience, she could hardly expect anything other than an unpleasant welcome. Renfru had been kind enough to warn her that she wouldn't be getting the red-carpet treatment.

He turned into a small courtyard dominated by a massive marble fountain. Evie followed warily. There were any number of places he could have hidden within the closed-off yard, and he could pounce on her at any moment. She edged into the court-yard, glamor still intact, and saw nothing. She moved farther inside, scanning the balconies overlooking the whispering foun-tain and seeking his thoughts with her mind. She was startled to find nothing. Seemed this demon was strong enough to block her.

Interesting.

When a strong, firm hand closed around her throat, Evie felt no fear. Even when the damned ugly demon came kissing-close to her face and bathed her with his fetid breath. This encounter was what she'd wanted. Although, maybe she hadn't wanted to end up in this particular position—held by the neck against a wall, a foot off the ground while her dead weight cut off the oxygen to her brain.

The hand at her throat didn't allow her to defend herself. Or *speak* in her defense. So drastic action was required, or she would be dead before she got any information from her captor. Evie shut her eyes and concentrated. A fullness spread along her back. Her shoulder blades rose and pressed against the skin of her back as her wings poked through the glamored slits in her upper back. In an instant, both Evie and Baa'ruk were enveloped by a pair of shimmering white and silver wings. Foot-long feathers sent wisps of silvery white dust floating around them.

She had hoped for a strong reaction. Perhaps the fear of God? Or maybe shocked, awed reverence.

Certainly not an ear-shattering fit of sneezing.

The head demon now stood, hands over his nose, mouth slightly open, eyes scrunched up in silent expectation of the next bout of ground-shaking sneezes. Little blades of grass peeking out from between the flagstones, shivered in the wake of his thunderous sneezes. Evie flapped her wings, which was unavoidable when folding them up behind her, and in a blink, both magnificent silver-tipped wings were gone.

Of course, she felt bad that she'd now started another fit of sneezes with a second breeze of wing dust. And of course, the whole thing wasn't really that funny especially when she'd so recently almost met her maker. But Evie couldn't help it. The first giggle that escaped her was tentative, mild. The next second she was having a full-blown giggle-fest.

At last, both sneezes and giggles faded into a calmer standoff, with Baa'ruk studying her with red, teary, amused eyes. His hand lay on the dagger at his belt, but the action now implied habit rather than threat. The red hue to his face, faded until his complexion returned to a natural milky colorlessness.

Baa'ruk had lost control of his glamor during his sneeze-fit and for the second time in one evening, Evie saw what truly lay behind a demon's glamor. But this time, what she saw made her feel strange. She'd seen glimpses of his true self when she had tailed him through the city streets, caught snatches of the pure white skin and pale blonde hair. Now, face-to-face with him, she remained amazed. And still uncertain how to assess her reaction. She wasn't repulsed at all.

Fascinated. That's what she was.

She reached out again, teasing his mind, trying to find a crack or little opening in his defenses but he was blocked solid. She gritted her teeth, annoyed.

In the background, the fountain trickled water from an upper bowl into a larger, lower one. The water would be tepid and unrefreshing, but the sound itself was cool.

Baa'ruk smirked, studying her as she stared at him.

"So, you got your eyeful. Satisfied?" A demon with self-esteem issues. Evie knew she'd need to tread carefully so she didn't take the bait.

"Will you let me talk now or would you like to just kill me and get it over with?" She crossed her arms and waited, knowing she was making herself vulnerable. Not that she wouldn't be able to defend herself, no problem there. Just that she'd prefer not to get damaged in the process.

Great. She was beginning to think like Ash.

She waited. Baa'ruk was bent over again, one finger under his nose as if he could possibly stop the next sneeze before he uttered it. Evie felt alarm surge thorough her. What would happen if he stalled one of those tremendous sneezes? Wouldn't the pressure explode his brain? Evie wasn't keen on getting sprayed with demon blood and brain. His next sneeze rocked the walls and sent plaster dust floating to the ground.

"You might as well talk and get out of here. I think I'm allergic to angels." He waved a hand at her to say what she wanted.

"Nephilim, actually."

Baa'ruk looked reasonably human again, although he shimmered now and then as if a breeze interfered with his glamor and shifted it a tiny bit, allowing her to see the creature within. Only one other thing stood out on Baa'ruk, more startling than his albinism. And perhaps because of his lack of color.

A swirling inky tattoo on his neck, which undulated on his skin like a living thing. It was some sort of script, so similar to the writing inscribed on the Seals that Evie shivered.

He raised a single eyebrow. "Nephilim. Angel. Whatever. You are the one responsible for killing so many of my people. I should actually kill you here and now on principle."

Evie stepped forward a single pace. Unseen feathers flapped around them and an equally invisible breeze blew silvery dust around them.

"Okay, okay, I see your point." He conceded, raised his hands in defense, and stepped back. "What is it you want?"

"What I don't want is to keep killing demons." That got Baa'ruk's attention easily enough. "What? Did you think I was here to eliminate you?"

"That's what you usually do with my kind." He shrugged, as if he didn't care, but his eyes were on her face, intent, watchful.

"Not because I want to. And not anymore." Evie scowled. The memory of the Irin Master's treachery still tore at her gut. He'd been using them. Why, she had yet to figure out. But it still pissed her off. "I need some information about a set of Seals inscribed with an unknown script. Funny enough, that script is remarkably similar to the writing on your neck." Evie stepped forward and inspected the demon's tattoo closely. The writing moved of its own accord just beneath his pearl-white skin. Creepy.

"The Seals." Baa'ruk's voice was a hushed and reverent whisper. He was oblivious to her inspection of his tattoos. But his words brought her back to the reason she was here.

"These Seals—what exactly are they?" Evie asked, her nose still inches away from Baa'ruk's neck.

"I can't tell you that." He was shaking his head. As if the very thought of revealing the purpose of the Seals would cause him to burst into a thousand hell-bound flames.

"You know, if you don't tell me, then more of your boys will bite it. It won't be me. But I don't have any control of it any more than the rest of my team." Evie frowned as she straightened and shook her head, still digesting the reality of the Irin Master's betrayal. She shuddered. Didn't much like the thought she had been his pawn over the last months.

She could still feel the weight of the Seal in her hand even though it was safely tucked away.

"Why do you want the Seals?" the demon asked.

"*I* don't want them, Barry. Someone else does, and I want to know why. And I want to stop him from getting them. Those Seals have cost too many lives. Demon and ethereal."

Baa'ruk glared, affronted at Evie's use of his human name. "I still don't think I can tell you just because you say you want to know."

"Fine, then. Someone I know already has four of your little rocks." Evie picked a number from the air and didn't add that she had two counting Renfru's, and Ling had one. "You can deal with them when they come visit for the rest of the Seals." She turned to leave.

"Wait." Baa'ruk took a small step toward her and stopped. "Who is it? Who wants the Seals?"

"First—what are they for?" Evie folded her arms, her eyes remaining on him, hard as obsidian.

He threw her a resigned glare. "They belong to Hades." He shook his head. "I can't believe I am actually telling you this, especially since you're the killer that's been offing my guys. But it was suspicious that only the Seal-Bearers were being eliminated."

"Seal-Bearers? So were they guarding the Seals?" Baa'ruk nodded. "How many Seal-Bearers are there?"

"Twelve, including me. There is only one whose identity I don't know." The demon studied Evie, the half-dreamy expression said he was remembering the majesty of her wings. "The Seals were protected. They cannot fall into the wrong hands. Way too powerful mojo."

"I had no idea there was a larger purpose until today." Evie could still feel the tingle of the disk in her fingers. "They sing, or have some sort of energy?"

It was that statement that shocked the demon more than even her wings had.

"You heard it sing?" At Evie's nod, he continued, "There are twelve Seals in total. Eleven Seals was charged to an Earth-side demon to protect until the Millennium of Service was over."

"Millennium of Service?" Evie was intrigued.

Baa'ruk scowled. "If you want me to tell you, then quit the chatter. Ask your questions later if you must." After one last glare, he said, "All twelve Seals are needed to mark the coming of the next Hades."

Evie opened her mouth to ask another question, then clamped it shut when Baa'ruk threw her a warning glare.

"The Seals of Hades form the gateway to the Underworld. Every millennium the Underworld becomes unstable. The balance of the Mother is shifted, and the Underworld falls into Chaos. New blood must complete the Rite of Passage, to assume the Throne of Hades for the next millennium. Hades must be good. Hades must be fair to rule the Underworld with heart and balance and justice. The Seals are hidden across the world, charged to the care of soldiers of the Underworld. The Seal-Bearers will guard the Seals with their lives, defend it to their deaths, for the Seals must not be possessed by evil."

Evie thought that was a bit of a contradiction, considering Hell is supposed to be essentially evil anyway.

"So only a good guy can be the King of the Underworld. That is so wrong!" Evie laughed. Then belatedly remembered she was supposed to shut up while the demon told his tale.

A look in Baa'ruk's direction revealed he was in fact finished talking.

"What about the twelfth Seal-bearer?" Evie asked.

The demon chief shook his head. "No idea. And it's probably safer that way."

Evie frowned and studied Baa'ruk's face, then decided he wasn't lying. "Okay, so what happens if a bad guy gets the Seals and become the next Hades?"

"Er...the shit hits the fan. Armageddon. End of Days. Put it any way you want but it's very, very bad news."

"What's the big deal?"

"The big deal, Nephilim, is the King of the Underworld controls the natural geology of the Earth. Volcanoes, earthquakes, tectonic plate activity." Baa'ruk raised his eyebrows. "You get the picture?"

Evie suppressed a shudder. "Okay, that is a big deal. So I get the job of making sure all the Seals are safe from the bad guy."

"Do you know who this guy is?" Suddenly Baa'ruk seemed very interested.

"I think I do, and now it's pretty clear why he's been having those awful tantrums when certain items never made it to him. It's like he knew when the demons were dead and when they got away." Evie frowned, talking more to herself than the demon, thinking back to each kill and Marcellus' urgent reaction to her kill confirmations.

"It's possible that he has the Tablet," Baa'ruk added, nodding almost to himself.

"Tablet?" Evie frowned.

"An ancient parchment with the names of every Earth-side

demon inked into it. Each time a demon is killed, the name disappears from the list." The expression on his face said he was not happy revealing that little tidbit either.

"Like a GPS for demon-kind?" Evie asked.

Baa'ruk grunted, not appreciating her humor. "Kinda. Specifically, for the Seal-bearers actually."

This was a lot to take in. Evie felt a bit shell-shocked. Now it sounded very much like Marcellus had every intention of finding all the Seals and claiming the position of King of the Underworld. Evie gritted her teeth. She'd known he'd been bad news all along. This just confirmed it.

"How do we stop him?" She looked at the albino demon, wondering if just maybe she could trust him.

"Make sure he doesn't get all the Seals." The demon studied Evie, a thoughtful lien to his features. "Tell me, were you sent to kill me?"

"No. I was sent by Renfru. He directed me to you. I told him to scram. Someone will come for him, especially now that you say the Tablet will tell the bad guys he's still alive." Renfru's boss grunted. "Cut him some slack. He refused to give me any information until I told him I'd killed Baltazar."

"You killed Baltazar?" Baa'ruk's eyes were wide with shock, and oddly enough, sorrow.

"Yes. He was my last target before Renfru. I was just doing my job, but something felt wrong about it." Guilt raised its head again.

"Probably the fact that Baltazar wouldn't have killed you before at least getting some answers from you." Baa'ruk's words were accusing as his blue veins pulsed beneath the white, almost translucent skin of his neck and face. His fists were clenched so hard the knucklebones were almost visible. It seemed poor Baltazar was going to be sorely missed. Now Evie felt worse than when she had actually killed him.

"I am truly sorry." Evie couldn't believe she was actually apologizing to Satan's spawn, but she had no choice. And he didn't seem to be very spawn-like either. Everything seemed to be happening around her, forcing her to act with the minimum of control. "If I'd known—"

The demon cut her off. "You need to collect all the Seals and take them back to Hades."

"Huh? You mean I need to take the Seals to the Underworld? Hell no!"

"Very funny." Baa'ruk rebuked her but smiled. At least he had a sense of humor. "It's the only way, unless you give them all to me."

"Now why would I do that?"

"I'll take it to Hades for you," he said with a smile.

"Sorry, but somehow I don't believe that. How do I know you won't take the Seals and make yourself the new King of the Underworld?"

"You don't. Nephilim, you cannot trust anyone. Not for this." Baa'ruk grabbed Evie by the shoulders and shook her. "Don't trust anybody. Once word gets out that so many of the Seal-Bearers are dead, every demon and his cousin will be looking for the Seals."

He moved a step back and reached inside his shirt, pulling out a thick lead chain. On its end hung another Seal. He tugged at it, breaking the links and freeing the Seal. "Take it," he said as he placed it in Evie's hands. "Take it and leave. Don't tell anyone that you have any of the Seals with you. Trust no one."

He squeezed her hands and looked deep into her eyes. Then he turned and began to walk away. He would have disappeared into the hot, humid New Orleans night. If she hadn't remembered something vital.

"Hey, Barry?"

He turned and gave her a questioning stare.

"I'll need a map then."

Baa'ruk stared at her, confusion knitting his colorless brow.

"Er...how do I get there? The Underworld?" She raised her eyebrow at him.

"Oh, yes. Right." Baa'ruk entered the courtyard again and led Evie to a white wooden door, the first of four identical doors on the ground floor of the building.

Darkness closed in on them within the room, but the demon didn't seem to care. Perhaps he had some power to see in the dark like the Nephilim. Another reminder that they may have more in common than was comfortable to consider. Rummaging in a drawer near the door, he retrieved a fountain pen and a serviette marked with a smudge of something red. Evie hoped it was ketchup.

When he handed her the napkin, she was surprised to see a cellphone number scrawled in a penmanship which belonged in the middle of the eighteenth century.

"Call me when you're ready. I'll fetch you. You will need to be ready in time to make it to the entrance by dawn. There is a window open at dusk and at dawn, only twice a day, so if you miss it, you will need to wait the day."

"Why are you doing this?" She studied his face, searching for a clue as to the reason why he was ready to help her when she'd killed so many of his people. She twisted the napkin in her hand and stared at his face.

"There's something about you that tells me you are the right one to protect the Seals. You and I still have a few scores to settle for my friends, but that can keep until the Seals are returned. We've hidden them long enough, and if someone out there is so desperate to find the Seals that they are now killing off the Seal-Bearers, then there is something going on here that's way bigger than just you and me." Baa'ruk walked to Evie and stared her straight in her eyes. "If you are the one, then you will succeed. Good luck. I shall await your call."

He walked Evie out into the courtyard where she left him

standing, looking slightly forlorn, bereft of his friends and now his precious Seal.

Evie rose in a magnificent flourish of wings and angel dust, ensuring she kept a safe distance from the demon. He inclined his head in an elegant, gracious nod and watched her as she hovered over the courtyard.

Then Evie turned and made for the estate.

CHAPTER 10

Back home from the bayou, Evie's head throbbed with a multitude of emotions. Confusion, concern, and suspicion warred within her. But all her thoughts ended up in one place. Why would Marcellus want the Seals of Hades? Did he really want to be Hades? And was that even possible or was the albino demon just messing with her head?

Evie was certain of only one thing—it was now imperative that she ensured the Master of the Irin did not get his grubby hands on all the Seals. Even if she hid a few of them from him, it would ensure he would be unable to perform the ceremony to transform himself into the new Hades.

She had to assume that was his goal and plan accordingly.

KNOCKING AT LING'S DOOR, Evie waited impatiently for her friend to open up. Ash answered and shoved it wider for Evie to enter. Ling sat on the bed, which was the only thing in the room that hadn't been turned upside down. The entire room looked much like a tornado had blazed through it. Tables and chairs were on their sides, cushions from the couch were upended and the stuffing ripped from them.

"What happened?" But Evie figured the question was moot.

"Marcellus and his army of looters, that's what. It must have happened while I was out." Ling was shaking her head, her face pale, but the skin at the corners of her eyes was tight. Ling appeared shaken but also angry.

Ash was just as upset. All color had drained from her cheeks so that she looked much like one of the white marble Apsara statues which graced numerous temple walls around India.

"Well, it's a good thing you didn't keep it here then," Evie said with a soft sigh. It was clear from the events of the last day that the Seals were the object of Marcellus' raids.

Ling nodded, rather more vehemently than she had intended, but the movement appeared to relax her. "You can say that again." Then she paused and gave Evie an odd look. "I don't know why, but I went to the armory and brought it with me." She patted her side, revealing the outline of a small bag which she'd strapped to her waist under her shirt.

Evie sighed. "That's good." The soft mattress gave as she sat beside Ling. She felt a bit awkward. It may not be prudent to try to comfort Ling, who had always professed to being anything but an emotional basket case. "Maybe you should keep it on you at all times."

"What if they search her?" Ash asked.

"Do you think they would dare?" Ling stood, her eyes flitting anxiously between the other two girls, hoping they'd both laugh off the possibility of a body search.

But Evie couldn't deny that Marcellus seemed to be getting more desperate. They could hardly rule out the possibility. "Maybe you should find a good hiding place for it. When you find out what it is, you won't be so keen to keep it too close to your body anyway."

"What is it?" Ling stared at Evie and frowned.

Evie hesitated.

"Look, Eves, you'd better tell me right this minute or so help me I might knock you out with the damned thing." Ling's grip tightened on the Seal, but Evie knew she didn't mean what she said.

"Okay, okay. Threats to my person will get you everything." Evie waved her hands in resignation. "Okay, so these disks are called Seals."

"Seals for what?" Ash butted in. "What are they for?"

"They are actually called The Seals of Hades."

The silence in the room was a palpable and shocked thing. Evie placed a finger beneath Ling's chin and lifted it slowly until the other girl's gaping mouth was closed.

"You'll start catching flies soon."

Ling clicked her tongue in annoyance. "What the hell are The Seals of Hades? It had better not be what I think it is."

"Trust me, it probably is."

EVIE BROUGHT the two shocked Nephilim up to speed on the Seals, their purpose, the Seal-Bearers and Baa'ruk's offer to help them.

"What we need is to make sure we have all the Seals and then you can call Barry." Ling confirmed what the other two girls were thinking.

"How do we find the rest of the Seals?" Ash asked, frowning and glaring at the Seal in Ling's grasp as if it were a coiled viper ready to strike.

"Marcellus might have them considering he's been sending us to every corner of the world for them. If he does, they may be hidden somewhere in his office." Evie voiced the plan, knowing the other two girls would not like it at all.

As they argued, Evie rose and began to pile the goose-down

stuffing back into the cushions of Ling's couch. She plumped the cushions up and pressed them back into the base of the seat. Two of the gold brocade cushions sported angry slashes on their once-beautiful surface. Evie walked around the room, keeping her hands busy, righting lamps and resetting drawers. There was nothing to be done for the curtains, so she dragged them off broken rods, which were now lying beneath the sill in a crumpled heap. She surveyed the damage, trying to tamp down her rising rage.

"Well, when you're done, my boots need polishing," remarked Ling.

Evie smiled and returned to the girls. "Sorry, I think better when I'm moving. So did you come up with a better plan?"

"Obviously not!" Ash snapped. "So how do we do this, then?"

"It has to be late. We have to make sure he won't be around. We can use our glamor but it's not a hundred percent. Who knows if he's using anti-glamor magic to ensure we don't break the rules." Evie wouldn't be surprised if he was using dark magic considering the company he kept. She looked at her two friends' faces, both strained and pale. "So you guys in? Time to back out is now."

The two girls nodded, then shook their heads in unison.

Ash and Evie rose to leave, when Ling said, "Hey, hold on."

Evie turned.

"Take this thing. I want none of it." She tossed it to Evie as if it were seeping deadly poison into her veins.

Evie reached out and caught it, already tensing her muscles for its weight. She tucked it beneath her clothes and left with Ash, leaving Ling to stare at the shambles of her room in dismay.

CHAPTER 11

Evie, Ling and Ash approached Marcellus' office in the dead of night. In his arrogance, Marcellus had omitted to alarm his office. Perhaps he'd assumed that his lackey Daniel would live within the walls of the room. Perhaps it was his intense sense of self-importance that allowed him to assume that nobody within the Irin would dare to trespass on his property.

And maybe that would have been the case in the past. But for Evie and her friends, everything changed the day Marcellus crashed into their rooms and violated their privacy.

"Are you sure he doesn't have an alarm or something?" Ash hissed into Evie's ear. Her friend's hot breath and the disturbance were both equally annoying. Rubbing her ear, she glared at Ash.

"Shush. What's the point in whispering when it's loud enough for the whole East Wing to hear you?"

Ash remained unaffected by the scolding merely glaring back at Evie and raising her eyebrows in further annoyance. "You convinced us this was a good idea. What if we get caught?"

"Ash, if you want to go back, now's your chance. Once we're inside, that's it." Evie looked over at Ling, who leaned against the wall on the other side of the large glass doors. She nodded silently, and Evie smiled and nodded at her, comforted by her friend's support. Now if only Ash would grow some guts. "Make up your mind, Ashika. We can't stand on this balcony forever."

Ash threw Evie a smoldering stare, tossed her braid over her shoulder, and thrust her shoulders back. "Fine. I'll shut up now."

Evie grinned and edged toward the doors. Both were closed, and the drapes were drawn. No light flickered from within but lack of it would pose no problem for any of the Nephilim. Evie pressed the handle and pulled the door open with infinite care.

Nobody breathed.

Each girl expected some sort of alarm to blare and to be surrounded by Marcellus' thugs.

Nothing happened.

The trio exchanged glances and relaxed.

Evie looked at each of her friends and made a masking motion over her face with her hand. They needed to glamor up. Once inside the glamor would protect them from being seen by any human who might enter the room. Evie hoped they would not be treated with any such intrusion.

Ready, the girls slid into the room, and plastered themselves against the doors behind the thick, dusty, velvet curtains. Evie parted the drapes and scanned the room.

Empty.

They slipped into the room, careful not to open the drapes too wide. Once inside, the girls began their search. All the Nephilim had a feline night-vision—only sharper, clearer. Drawers opened in silence and papers were ruffled as they worked. They edged around the room, methodically searching every drawer, nook and cranny.

At last, they met in the center of the room and stared at each other in frustration and disappointment. Evie hung her head, upset with herself as well for endangering her friends. Ash grabbed her arm and shook it, pointing at the door the balcony, mouthing the words "Let's go."

Evie was about to agree when she stiffened with shock and snapped her head back down to look at the floor. Beneath their feet was a round rug, an intricate tapestry woven into it. The images of nine rings were woven within the fabric. Nine, not eight but close enough, A coincidence? Evie shivered. Nine rings. Had it been here right beneath their feet all along, masked by the fading threads?

Slowly the girls stepped off the carpet, and Evie shoved it aside with her foot. Beneath the carpet, nothing struck them as out of the ordinary—just long panels of oak flooring. Evie pressed the floorboards with her foot, testing the wood for any area that felt different to her weight. The slight squeak of the floorboard announced a loose board, and Evie dropped to her knees. She grasped her knife from its scabbard and slipped its slim blade into the space between two loose boards. A little upward leverage popped the board out to reveal a dark, musty space filled with numerous wrapped objects.

Evie understood the need to wrap them. They had the tendency to sing a loud musical song if they came into contact with anything hard. Evie could only imagine the noise they would make if two of those Seals touched each other. All three girls quickly sifted through the dark pile. They didn't have the time or the luxury of opening each parcel and confirming it as a Seal. It didn't take long before the space was almost empty. Three packages were much smaller and she felt certain they were not Seals, but she grabbed them anyway. For them to be hidden away with the Seals meant Marcellus believed they were important.

Ling placed the floorboard back, tucking it into place in utter silence. Evie toed the rug into place turning it so it sat in the same direction she'd first noticed it. No sense in alerting Marcellus or Daniel that something was different.

No sooner had the rug returned to its original position did the sound of a key in the door's lock reverberate through the room as loud as a gunshot. Hands weighed down with their tiny burdens, the girls scrambled back behind the curtain and out the door. Evie shut it as quietly as she could, using her elbow to depress the handle. They tucked the packages into every available pocket, raced for the balustrade and leaped over, no time to check for the Night Guard. A millisecond later three sets of wings were brandished in a muffled puff of feathers and feather dust. The girls flew west, around the building, remaining below the third floor. Probably Daniel entering the room at this late hour, but Evie preferred not to be the one to find out.

BACK IN EVIE'S ROOM, they tipped the contents of each package onto the bed. In total Marcellus had managed to accumulate seven Seals—four large and three smaller ones. Along with Evie's three and Ling's one, they had a total of eleven Seals-eight large and three small. Evie frowned.

"That's strange. The seals have nine emblems engraved on the surface with each seal having a different emblem engraved much larger than the others. But we have eleven in total." She moved them around on the bed until eight sat in a perfect circle. But there were nine on Marcellus' carpet, the patterns of which were an echo of the engravings on the Seals themselves. Were they missing a Seal?

Three smaller disks—merely large fat coins—were left. None of these disks had engravings which matched the other eight. One pair bore the engraving of an eye and a hand. The last one had three heads inscribed into it. The first head faced left, the middle one looked straight ahead and the third faced to the right.

"How odd." Ling was the first to remark on the three Seals' strangeness.

Evie sat on the bed and moved her hand to push aside her knife only to find the scabbard light . . . and empty.

"Shit. Shit . . . ." Evie swore and stamped her foot. "Idiot. Stupid, foolish idiot."

The other two girls stared at Evie in confusion.

"What?" Evie barely heard Ling's questions, so engrossed was she in her self-recrimination. "Evie, shut up."

Evie groaned. "My knife...]I must have left it on the floor when I levered the floorboard open. Damn it. It must have been right at my feet and we probably threw the rug over it. Damn. Whoever entered the room when we left is going to see it soon enough. I have to go back for it."

"Are you crazy?" Ash stood up and grabbed Evie by both arms. "That's suicide. If you get caught, Marcellus will have the right to banish you, or worse."

"I have to at least try to get it back. If anyone finds it, I'll be in deep trouble anyway. I can't believe I was so stupid. I never set my knife down, ever."

"You were preoccupied. We all were." Ling tried to reassure Evie. "Look, you do need to get it back. What do we do with these Seals in the meantime?"

Evie's eyes fell on the bed, which now seemed weighed down by the gleaming Seals.

"Leave them, I'll find a place to stash them." Evie's first thoughts were of the warning issued by Baa'ruk. He'd been so insistent, so urgent that fear trilled through her at the very thought of anyone finding out that they were now in possession of all the Seals.

But while Evie spoke, Ling's eyes remained trained on the Seals, almost entranced. Ash and Evie both looked at each other. Ash moved toward Ling, linking arms with her friend and dragging her to the door. "C'mon. We'd better head off to bed and get some rest. If we pitch up to morning classes looking like we've been partying hard all night, someone will get super suspicious as soon as Marcellus finds he's been robbed."

Ling nodded and walked out. Ash's eyes were lined with worry as she closed the door behind her.

Evie wasted no time in re-wrapping each Seal and taking the packages to the chimney. She felt for the space and tested the bricks on either side of the little cavity. Only one was slightly loose. After a few minutes of gently jimmying the brick, it finally dropped out, a shower of brick dust raining down on the wood arranged below. Evie packed the Seals in tightly, thankful they fit well enough not to threaten to fall out of their hidey-hole. She was tempted to keep the three smaller coins with her but thought better of it.

Evie reached for her phone, sending a quick text to tell Baa'ruk she was ready. Seconds later she got a response, confirming their meeting at three thirty. She raced back to the Master's office. Evie had wasted enough time stashing the Seals. For all she knew, Daniel and Marcellus had discovered the robbery and were both going berserk.

 $\mathcal{E}$ vie hurried back to Marcellus' office, using the same route they'd used to get in earlier. On the balcony, she listened at the glass, straining to catch even the faintest sounds. She heard nothing.

She threw a cloak of glamor over her, and cracked open the door, hoping to slide in quickly. Footsteps drew close to the curtain and Evie held her breath, shutting the door as quietly as possible. She plastered herself against the wall. Someone walked to the curtain and thrust the two drapes aside, reaching for the handle and shoving open the door.

Marcellus stepped out onto the balcony and walked to the edge, looking left and right furtively. He was looking for something or someone.

Evie's heart clenched.

Did he know the Seals were gone?

If not, what could he be looking for?

Evie shook away the paranoia and used the opportunity to enter the room while the curtain flapped from the disturbance. Keeping to the wall beside the balcony door, Evie scanned the floor near the rug, desperation making her stomach roll with nausea.

There. Under Marcellus' desk, the knife lay gleaming.

A silent, shiny threat to Evie's very life.

One of them must have kicked it in their hurry to leave. A step forward and she had to halt in her tracks as Marcellus bustled into the office and pulled the door shut behind him. Evie's heart sank when he withdrew a key from his pocket and locked the door.

Damn.

Now her escape route was officially out of service. First things first. Evie had to retrieve the dagger, then think about how she was going to escape from the room. Marcellus went to his desk and seated himself, a cunning, cold smile wrapped around his face. He opened a large, ancient tome and began to read, making notes as he went.

Evie moved forward an inch at a time, taking pains to avoid the rug, which hid the now empty hole in the floor. She managed to stay off the squeaky floorboard beneath the round rug.

Then her foot came down on another loose board and the wood squealed like a pig, the sound loud and coarse in the silent room. Marcellus' head snapped up. He looked straight at Evie, and it creeped her out. She had to reassure herself that he couldn't see her. The glamor was strong.

Calm down.

As he rose, she took a few steps forward toward his desk and the dagger.

She'd been paying attention to her distance to the dagger, and when the floorboard creaked again behind her, she turned in slowest of motion. To come nose-to-nose with Marcellus.

He can't see you. Calm down.

"Who's there?" Marcellus voice now held a hint of steel.

Evie didn't answer.

She had enough potential troubles. Now she held her breath.

If she breathed on him, he'd know he had company. The warmth of her breath would be clue enough that someone was with him in the room. He seemed to sense Evie as he scanned the room and came back to the spot in front of him. Only when he stepped forward again did Evie realized he was standing on the spot of the creaking board. Evie stood a foot away from her dagger.

Almost there. Patience.

Marcellus stood in silence. Listening. Waiting. Evie stayed still right in front of him.

He tested the board a few times, then eventually returned to his desk, having tired of his vigil at the squeaky board. Evie took that opportunity to grab the blade and slip it silently back into the scabbard at her side.

Now to find another way out of the room.

Evie's breaths came in short silent puffs as she watched Marcellus at his desk. He looked up intermittently, scanning the room then returning to his reading. He'd have to have been dead not to feel Evie's eyes on him. The large room felt the size of a toilet stall, and Evie clamped down on spasms deep within her lungs. Hyperventilating now would be a very bad thing. He couldn't see her. That was enough.

She had made her way to about ten steps away from the door so far. Each step was agonizing, muscles tightening and cramping as she took one slow-motion step at a time. Ball to heel, ball to heel, slowly does it. Thankfully, no more floorboards creaked as she made progress to the door. Never mind what she would need to do once she got to the door. Evie concentrated on getting there first.

Worry about the hard stuff later.

She turned to check on Marcellus. And stared straight into his eyes. His face was inches from hers. In fact, he was so close her chest would have touched his if he moved the tiniest step forward. She would have gasped in shock if he hadn't put a hand out. She took a few steps back, her heart thudding. Like a blind man searching for an impediment, he reached into the air in front of him, fingers outstretched and skeletal.

He swiped wide and missed Evie's face by a finger's breadth. The added shock of his hand moving toward her cut off any sound from her throat. She ducked slowly, dropping into a crouch, careful not to make any fast movements which would disturb the air in any way. The guy must have some amazing senses to still be bugged by Evie's invisible presence in the room. He stood there, hands now on his hips, scanned the air, a frown marring his pale forehead.

"What are you doing staring into space?" Daniel's voice rang out. Marcellus and Evie turned to Daniel, who stood in the open doorway, surprise and curiosity filling his face. Evie, from her position at ankle level, was hidden from the doorway by a bank of filing cabinets. She craned her head to watch Marcellus—just in case he decided to trample her to death.

"Just daydreaming." Marcellus covered his gaffe.

"There are better things to do with your time, don't you think?" Daniel said coldly. But Evie was puzzled. His voice lacked any of his usual kowtowing deference to Marcellus. In fact, the table seemed strangely reversed with Marcellus the one affecting the respectful tone.

How very interesting.

But Evie could waste no time contemplating their strange behavior. With the door wide open, she saw her opportunity for freedom right in front of her. She moved, silent as a cat, rounding the wooden cabinets and heading for the door still in a crouch. As luck would have it, Daniel decided at that particular second to join Marcellus where he stood still contemplating the empty air in front of his face.

Evie was forced to dive out of Daniel's way to avoid a collision with him. She missed him by an inch, overcompensated and almost tipped herself onto the floor. Thankfully, she was close to the floor and placed a supporting hand on the carpet. Daniel turned and seemed to lock eyes with Evie, whose heart thundered with fear.

Can he see me? No, silly, He can't. No human can see a Nephilim in glamor. Calm down.

A closer look and it was clear he couldn't see her. His eyes were slightly unfocussed, as if he was looking at something behind Evie.

"It is done." Marcellus' voice broke their concentration and Daniel's attention was redirected to the Master. Evie took the opportunity to hightail it out of the room. Once outside she paused and waited.

What was done?

"Good. Did you make it look natural?" Evie imagined Marcellus nodding in the silence that followed. "At last that particular obstacle has been removed. Now we can get on with it."

"We just need the rest of the Seals—" The door slammed shut, cutting off the rest of the conversation. The room must have been soundproofed as Evie was unable to hear what they were saying no matter how close she thrust her ear to the door.

Frustrated, she backed away. At least she had the Seals and they'd soon get the surprise of their lives when they discover they now needed eleven Seals.

She hurried to see Patrick. What would he say about her discoveries? She hoped he wouldn't be too disappointed in her.

Evie ached for some kind of release from her confusion. Yesterday, Patrick had refused to acknowledge anything was wrong even though she had seen his face, seen the disk had been of grave concern to him. But he'd remained so calm about it.

What could possibly be his reason for not helping her find out more about Marcellus and his plans for the Brotherhood? He was ill, but she'd never known Patrick to back down from a challenge. And now that she had the Seals in her possession, all she wanted was for Patrick to tell her she'd done the right thing. But what if he thought it was a bad idea?

Not that she could return the Seals anyway.

She'd slowed her pace on the way to speak to him. Would it be too late to talk to him? But it was just on three in the morning and her rendezvous with Barry was not far off. Patrick's immortality had not lessened the requirements of the human body, he still needed sleep and food like any normal person. As did Evie and the other Nephilim.

Unlike angels, their humanity demanded they care for their fragile bodies. If their bodies gave out, they had no option to find another one. Although most Nephilim were long-lived, it was a common misconception that nothing could kill them.

Evie tapped her knuckles on the door, but the knock sounded flat as the door swung open with the pressure. Why was Patrick's room door left open? He valued his privacy, especially now that he was so frail. He rarely accepted visits from the students either.

Alarm lifted the hairs on the back of her neck.

She pushed the door open with her toe as her hand went to her side to retrieve her blade, glad she had taken the time to retrieve the weapon. Evie stepped quietly into the room, pulling her glamor over her to conceal her presence. In case an intruder still lurked within Patrick's room, she'd be able to catch them in the act.

She wasn't sure what she expected to see, but when her eyes fell on Patrick she knew what she had sensed even before she'd entered the room.

An icy cold filtered through Evie as she stepped toward the bed, fingers of grief closing slowly around her heart.

Death's pallor had touched the room throughout Patrick's convalescence, but tonight it hung thick and suffocating within the room. Fingers of moonlight snaked across the room and stopped at the foot of the bed as if afraid to reach any farther, leaving the hideous four-poster in murky shadows.

Even before she reached his bedside, Evie knew the hand she touched would be cold and lifeless. Her fingers grazed his knuckles. Ice bled into her blood. She gulped down a grief-ridden sob. Cold seeped into her body as if the simplest touch of Patrick's flesh soaked up the iciness of his skin, progressing through her limbs and turning her blood to shards of ice.

She turned her attention to the room then, eyes hot, vengeance brimming in her soul. Evie searched every nook and cranny, even inside the closets. Lastly, she opened the glass doors and checked the length of the balcony. Only after she was certain there was nobody in the room did she slumped down beside her father, teacher, and friend.

This time he didn't sneak a peek at her through half-shut eyes. Didn't smile that benevolent smile he reserved for only her.

Tears burned her throat and ran unchecked down Evie's cheeks. Though she made no sound as she sobbed, Evie was screaming inside. The terrible, wailing, heart-wrenching scream of familial loss and despair.

CHAPTER 13

Evie sat next to Patrick's body in the silence and the shadows. She felt the bleak cold of the encroaching morning seep into her. The icy touch of Patrick's hand within hers seeped all the way to her heart. Although his health had been steadily getting worse, Evie had never allowed herself to contemplate what she would do when his illness finally conquered him.

She stared at his face through a sheen of tears. He didn't have anything to tell her after all. No advice, no reprimands. And worst of all, no goodbyes.

At last, when her fingers were cramped and as cold as Patrick's, and when her shoulders began to burn, she moved. Evie laid Patrick's hands on his chest and smoothed the covers around him. His eyes were closed. He'd always joked about the coins. Always kept the two confederate silver coins in his bedside drawer just in case.

He'd laughed about it and so had Evie. Now they would come in handy.

Although it had been bandied about as a joke, Evie suspected that Patrick really did believe in the tradition. He would want her to place the coins on his eyes—his payment to Charon.

She leaned over, pulled open the drawer and rifled around for the silver pieces. Coins in hand, she nudged the drawer closed and turned to place them on Patrick's eyelids when she stiffened with shock. The rubbing of the Seal was gone. Patrick had taken the copy on the piece of fine paper, folded it carefully and placed it on the table beside his water glass. Now it was nowhere to be seen.

Something glinted on the floor between the table and the bed. Evie fell to her knees and peered closer. Patrick's crystal water glass now lay on the floor, half hidden by the bed-covers. Puzzled, she gripped the lip with two fingers and dragged it toward her. Sitting back, she turned the glass around in her hand and hissed with pain. She withdrew her hand sharply as blood welled from the edge of her fingers. The shattered lip had sliced into two of Evie's fingers leaving her with a pair of deep, jagged cuts.

She rose and rifled through Patrick's closet for a handker-chief, quickly wrapping it around the cuts. She pressed down hard to stem the flow of blood, then sat on the bed to contem-plate the discovery of the broken glass.

What had happened to cause him to drop the glass with such force that the crystal would shatter at the lip? Had it fallen from Patrick's hand, it would have fallen heavy-bottom side down. Naturally the bottom of the glass would have been damaged, not the lip.

Further searching and Evie came up empty. No sign of the rubbing and no further clues about the broken glass. She'd searched a second time, more for reassurance than thoroughness. She hoped to find the chipped piece of crystal. That at least would have given her a clue as to how the glass had broken. She stood at the foot of the bed, staring at Patrick's unmoving body, feeling hopeless and helpless. Everyone had said Patrick was coming to the natural end of his life. And here—

Evie gasped.

Did you make it look natural?

She'd heard that phrase not so long ago. Not long ago, Daniel had asked Marcellus if he'd made "something" look natural. Could they have had something to do with Patrick's death?

Evie's gut spasmed, and her instinct screamed. She'd known all along Marcellus was instrumental in Patrick's illness. This just confirmed it. But what could she possibly do about it? It wasn't as if she could bang their door down and have them thrown in jail for murder. Here in the Brotherhood, Marcellus was judge, jury, and executioner.

The room faded into darkness. A cloud hid the weak moon on the horizon and took away the bare light. Evie stood still in the darkness and made a decision.

She could do nothing here. But she could make sure the bastard never sets his eyes on the Seals.

There had been a niggling doubt about whether she was doing the right thing taking the Seals but now, sitting on Patrick's bed, beside his cold corpse, she was sure. Baa'ruk would be waiting to take her to the entrance to Hades.

She was now the Guardian of the Seals of Hades. And she had to protect them with her life.

Patrick would approve. She had to believe he would approve. Had to believe he would give her his blessing. Before the cloud-cover receded, Evie left the room, leaving the door ajar as she'd found it.

She had a demon waiting.

She had work to do and now there was no reason to wait.

BACK IN HER ROOM, Evie retrieved the Seals from their hiding place and stuffed them into her backpack, taking extra care to ensure that each disk was well wrapped. The last thing she wanted was to have the Seals knock against each other and announce to the world that she had the dreaded things in her possession.

The room lay silent behind her. Empty. Her eyes filled with tears. For Patrick. For herself. For everything she was likely to lose. Friends. Her purpose with the Irin.

Evie felt like she was saying good-bye. It wasn't as if she was leaving for good, though. She just had no idea what was in store for her. Maybe they wouldn't find the entrance, or maybe she wouldn't need to cross the River. Maybe she could return the Seals to Hades and come home, and everything would be okay. For now, she had to get a move on.

But what if Barry didn't come?

Pull yourself together. He'll be there, and all this will be over soon.

Evie's laugh was silent and bitter. When it was all over she'd be back under Marcellus' thumb and back to normal. Back to being without Patrick and to watching Marcellus control the Warriors. But there was no turning back now. Best to get out before Daniel and the Master find they were missing their Seals.

Not to mention missing a Nephilim.

There'd be hell to pay and Evie intended to be as far away from the fireworks as possible. She shut the door and tiptoed past the other rooms. Ling and Ash would be asleep and snoring their way to dawn. The temptation to rouse them from their beds and take them with her was almost overwhelming. She would have loved the company. But she conceded it was safer to leave her friends at home. She'd never be able to live with herself if anything happened to them. They would have been just as eager as she was to take this journey, especially since it meant thumbing a nose at Marcellus.

But Evie had to do this herself. By killing Patrick, Marcellus had taken this beyond the line. Marcellus had attacked her family and for Nephilim, vengeance overpowered all else.

This was her fight.

Return the Seals, come back, and hold Marcellus and Daniel accountable for the death of her family.

Slipping out through the darkened kitchen, Evie watched for the guards. A dark, imposing figure tramped past and Evie held her breath until he disappeared around the far corner of the building. With the coast clear she scrambled through the herb garden and fruit trees which grew all the way to the back end of the estate. The pungent scent of thyme, rosemary, and chives assaulted her nostrils as her jogging feet broke leaves and released the aromas to the silent morning air.

Every few seconds she paused behind a tree trunk, listening for footsteps. Expecting any minute to hear the crashing of booted feet on the soft ground—Marcellus' mob in pursuit of the Seal thief.

The grounds were large, taking her at least fifteen minutes to make her way to the electric fence that wrapped around the Irin land. At the fence Evie thrust out her wings in a flash of feathers and flew over. It was more of a winged leap rather than a short flight and she landed on the other side in a swoosh of retracting wings.

A deep, soft cough echoed among a copse a few feet in front of Evie. The bushes rustled and blond dreads poked through the branches. Relief cooled Evie's heated brow.

"Hi," she whispered and crouched down beside him. She kept her personal space clear around her, still slightly unnerved with Barry the albino demon, secretly relieved that he'd actually kept his word.

"Hi. You're in the clear." He nodded at the darkened estate. "Nobody followed you. We'd better get going."

Evie took one last forlorn look at her home, before Baa'ruk led her to the other side of the copse. Hidden beneath a fall of branches and dead leaves, was a sleek, black motorcycle.

Evie's eyebrows shot up into her hairline. "What in Heaven's name are you doing with a Ducati?" She was in awe.

"Heaven had nothing to do with it." Baa'ruk smiled at her and tossed a shiny black helmet at her. "We have to make a living while Earth-side. And the boss prefers we stay away from illegal stuff. I'm a mechanic."

Evie's fingers stuck to the helmet in hands suddenly slick with sweat. There was only one bike. How do you ride any motorcycle without holding onto the driver? She suppressed the urge to shudder, grateful for the darkness which cloaked her prejudice.

"We'd better get going." Baa'ruk tossed a booted, leather-clad leg over the bike and sat, waiting for Evie to hop on behind him.

"How come you just don't disapparate there?" she asked. Anything else besides this.

"Because within the Underworld, all forms of magic which do not belong to Hades have no power."

"Oh," was all Evie could manage while intensely aware of the demon's thickset body right in front of her. The machine roared to life and jerked forward. Evie—with no choice left—clung to Baa'ruk's padded jacket, thankful for its thickness. She gripped the fabric instead of hugging his torso to hold on.

With the helmet snug around her head, she was unable to ask where exactly they were going. The bike implied it would be nearby. Well, nearby for someone who could easily traverse the length of the US in one night. She considered the very possible option of flying Baa'ruk to the location. But she was stumped again. Flying meant she'd have to hold on to the demon, hold him far too close for her liking.

She'd rather make out with Flash than be that close to a demon.

Evie smiled, slightly ashamed. Flash was a good guy, nothing wrong with him in the make-out department, either. She was being unfair to bring him into the equation. And although she was far from interested in Flash as a canoodling partner, he would be a fairly nicely packaged, good-looking option.

She concentrated on holding on.

Holding on meant getting away. For now, Evie just wanted to be as far away from Greylock as possible when the disappearance of the Seals was discovered.

CHAPTER 14

Baa'ruk the demon rider sped into the Appalachians. The only sound on the quiet morning road was the voluptuous roar of the engine. They hung a right and sped into the foothills. Soon they were surrounded by trees and greenery, a good place to hide especially since the sun would soon make its appearance over the horizon. Evie scanned the clear skies. It was going to be a glorious day.

As the bike sped away from Greylock, taking Evie farther away from her dead mentor, she thought her pain would get easier. But grief still twisted its knife deep into Evie's heart. Would someone have found Patrick by now? Probably Castor. Evie could almost hear Castor's keening cry. Her heart ached for him. Another thing they would both share.

Now they would both be alone again.

And hour later Barry slowed, turning off the road into a stand of trees. He parked the bike out of sight of the road and said, "Let's have something to eat. It's been one helluva morning."

Evie was amazed that the demon had the forethought to pack a bag of food for the trip. Amazing that he had been so thoughtful. More amazing that she herself had totally forgotten her own stomach. Food had been the last thing on Evie's mind.

Barry's stale beignets filled the emptiness in her stomach, taking away the gnawing hunger, but leaving behind a queasiness that made Evie wonder if she would be able to keep the food down. She flailed about for something to think about other than Patrick, and Castor's lonely grief.

"You coming with me?" she asked Baa'ruk as she tidied away the remnants and crumbs, throwing her paper cups into a nearby trashcan.

"What? Are you kidding? Not to Hades—no way!" The demon laughed, his pale eyes crinkled and white teeth glittered in the weak dawn light. He had no need for his glamor this morning. Had shed it in totality.

"Why not? Don't you want to visit home? Or do you Earth-side demons have a no-return policy?" she jibed.

"Don't you know anything about the Underworld?" he asked in disbelief.

"Why would I be an expert on the Underworld? I have no interest in Hell as a vacation spot, thanks much!" Her lips twisted wryly.

"Hades, the Underworld, is the world of the dead. The shades. The spirits. The accursed. Demons live in Hell. We are very much alive in case you haven't noticed, that is until you kill us...."

Baa'ruk smiled, taking the edge off the accusation. Nevertheless, it did hurt. Her whole Warrior life had been based on the tenet of "shoot now ask questions later." The problem was she was a crack shot. None ever survived long enough to answer any questions.

"We are children of the darkness, not of the dead."

"Yeah, I know. You are children of the Angels just like me." She laughed drily, unable to keep the distaste from her voice.

"Laugh all you want. It's the truth. You think appearances make you what you are?" Evie blushed, ashamed that she sounded like a superficial airhead. "A good few of us were Earth-side for centuries, guarding the Seals."

"Why not just hide them someplace together?"

"Because together, the Seals generate a power. Like a beacon. Certain interested parties have the tools to find them. That's why we need to keep moving and get you to the entrance fast." Baa'ruk had kept one eye on the road through the entire conversation.

"Fine with me. The sooner I hand them over to his Lordship, the sooner I can get back home to my life." Evie dusted her hands on her butt and pulled her helmet back on, fastening the buckle under her chin. This time, when she jumped on behind Baa'ruk, she forgot that she should have been totally grossed out at being so close to a demon.

THE DUCATI PURRED, then grumbled to a stop. Evie tugged off the helmet and ran her fingers through her hair as she slid off the motorcycle. They were standing at the base of a mountain in the middle of the Appalachians. Rocks spilled down it as if a giant's kid had tossed their marbles onto the side of the mountain, letting them fall haphazardly to the ground.

Baa'ruk began to walk up the incline and Evie followed. She considered hovering, giving her wings a turn. Then thought better of it. The last time she'd shucked her wings out in the vicinity of her demon companion, he'd gone into a sneezing fit. A demon engrossed in a fit of sneezes would be of no real use to her. Better not to incapacitate her guide.

They had climbed a few yards up the hill when Baa'ruk stopped. Evie stopped short of walking right into his back. She peered over his shoulder. The dark mouth of a cave beckoned, set into the rock face so strategically that unless you knew where to find it, you would pass it by a hundred times without seeing it.

"You can't see it from the ground at all." Evie huffed, only slightly out of breath from the climb.

"No. You can't see it at all unless you know what you're looking for. It's glamored as well." Evie wasn't surprised. It didn't hurt to take precautions. Besides, she didn't think Hades would appreciate unsuspecting hikers tumbling down into his world uninvited.

As much as she herself was uninvited, she came to Hades bearing gifts. Though he may not want the Seals back, at least he'd know what to do with them.

"Okay, so once I get through the cave, where am I going?" Evie felt her heart rate spike now that the time to descend into the bowels of the Earth was finally at hand.

"A small river will lead you out of the cave and will take you to the Styx. The underground river beneath this cave feeds the Styx."

"Still not coming?" Evie tried one last time, smiling at Baa'ruk. He shook his head. "So will you be in deep crap with your boss?"

"The boss will understand once I explain what happened." He nodded, clearly trying to convince himself with his words. Evie hoped he would be okay. One stray thought ran through her mind. What if this was just a huge plot to kidnap a Nephilim? And she would have walked right into it.

Evie shook her head and her doubts dissipated.

"Oh, before I forget. Could you get a message to someone for me?" When Baa'ruk nodded she asked him to let Castor know where she was going and why. She hated the thought of him worrying about her. The demon chieftain seemed happy to help her and Evie smiled at him, still finding it strange that she couldn't put Barry in a neat little box called 'Evil murderous hell-born creature'. Somewhere along the way he'd become a person to her. How strange.

Evie blinked and brought herself to the present. She held out her hand and said, "Thanks, Barry. For everything." The demon took it, giving it a brisk, embarrassed shake.

"Off you go now, and remember what I said. And be careful. Don't talk to the shades and don't stop to help anyone. Get to Charon and cross the river. Eat nothing, drink nothing, and stay out of the water. And be safe." Baa'ruk's spiel came to a sudden stop as if he'd run out of gas.

"Thanks." Evie set off with a wave at the pale demon who stood at the mouth of the cave like a ghost, shimmering like a mirage. He had a strange look on his face, a mix of worry and pride, a father sending his kid off to war or something. Evie shook her head. She must have been seeing things.

In the bright morning light, it was easy to ignore the stark truth. Evie was about to descend into the depths of the Underworld. Back home, in her room, this reality had been a mere possibility.

Now she stood at the threshold, literally and figuratively.

The cave mouth yawned ahead of her. The entrance, the size of the average doorway, was carved out of the rock. Closer inspection made it clear that the job was not natural. Too neat, the edges too smooth. In reality, the cave was a tunnel just high enough to accommodate Evie's height and probably wide enough to allow the robust Baa'ruk to pass.

Evie called her angel-light instinctively. It flickered for a moment then faded, plunging the tunnel back into suffocating darkness. Evie groaned.

No magic allowed in Hades.

Then she grinned. Fortunately, she had come prepared. She pulled her bag from her shoulder and rummaged inside until her fingers touched the rubber casing of her flashlight. It had never been used, always there just in case.

Now the bright light glowed ahead of her, sufficient to guide her slowly along the tunnel as it gradually widened into a cave.

The walls soon grew slick with moisture and the air dense and thick. The floor of the tunnel took on a steady downward slope.

Evie walked for a long time without any change in her surroundings. The floor still sloped down. Only her ears felt the pressure of the descent as they began to pop. After what seemed like a couple hours of walking, the track leveled off and opened into a wider cave than the one she'd entered through.

Water trickled somewhere in the cavern and Evie looked around, seeking the source of the eerily disembodied sound. At her left, a thin stream fell over a rocky outcrop, tumbling into a small pond. From the pond, the water cut a path in the rock and snaked out of the cave along the wall. Evie followed it, her boot-heels echoing on the hard stone as she walked. The stream meandered into a dull light at the cave's entrance.

Outside again, Evie shaded her eyes automatically. She needn't have bothered. The light was not from any kind of sun. The sky above was dark, strangely similar to the average Earth-side night sky.

Just no stars.

And although the sky was dark, and no moon shone its light upon Evie, a dull light glowed and lit the narrow exit of the cave. It also threw stark light onto the barren valley below.

CHAPTER 15

Evie tucked the flashlight back into her bag and picked her way carefully down the hillside. Barry's words echoed in her ears as she stumbled down the rocky embankment. The slope spilled down the rugged bank to a valley split in two by the formidable River Styx. The stream originating in the cave now ran alongside Evie, bubbling cheerfully, clearly not understanding it was making its way down to the river of the dead.

The landscape was a curious combination of black waters, red shale, and iron-gray rocks. At the horizon, gray and murky blue hinted at an impending dawn.

What kind of dawn would it be without the sun?

Evie suppressed a shiver. She was alone down here and had to be super careful. One wrong move and she'd never see her friends again, let alone another real sunrise.

The path proved precipitous and Evie slowed down to a shuffle as she made her way to the valley below. It was slow going and she paused. From her position, the panoramic view should have been breathtaking.

But the river ran morosely by, almost black and insidious, like a slimy black viper, slithering along the valley floor. Evie would not have been surprised to learn the blood of the dead gave the river its dismal hue.

The entire valley lay barren. No plants, no bushes. Just trees which may have died centuries ago and now stood waving bare, gray-brown arms, an air of solitude and menace so incongruous yet so appropriate.

Desolation weighed her down, slowed her steps. An inexplicable foreboding shriveled her tongue to a sandpaper crisp. The barren land was frigid. No breeze blew, no sun warmed the rocks and stones carpeting the valley. Evie's thigh muscles clenched.

A silent urge to turn and run.

To leave this place. Perhaps someone else would sort this whole mess out and she could go back to her normal life. But Marcellus' words echoed in her head.

It is done.

Her gut twisted. Patrick was dead and Marcellus had orchestrated it. What else did he have in store for the followers of the Brotherhood? And more importantly, what would he do if he were in possession of the Seals? Marcellus would not make a good ruler of the Underworld. Barry's eloquent statement was more than enough confirmation.

Hades must be a good guy.

Momentum and Evie's feet pulled her down the slope until she was standing and staring at the river running thick and dark past her. The depths of the water swirled with color. Here and there splotches of brown, white, and gray slid past as fast as the river could take them. It took precious minutes for Evie to accept the strange shapes were bodies. Eyes staring, mouths screaming in silence, they floated by, arms raised forever—pleading for release from their own endless death. A pale hand broke the surface of the water with a splash. A wizened, ancient face followed the hand which grabbed onto the bank with bitter, gnarled fingers.

"Help me! Help me please!" Those eyes glistened, and even

though Evie knew he'd just risen from the water, she was convinced they were filled with tears.

The water stank. Of putrid flesh and death. Despite the stench, the odor of decay and rot attracted not a single fly.

Drawn to his pleas, she leaned forward. Her fingers reached out to grasp the man's hand and pull him free from the imprisoning water.

The loud caw of a raven snapped her back to reality and she fell back, aware again of her surroundings. A surge of despair swept over her. How easily she'd been entranced by the man's pleas. How easily she had lost her sense of self-preservation.

Evie steeled her mind and heart against the cries and forced herself to walk along the bank, away from the pleading man and toward a small stone outcropping pretending to be a pier. She stood silently, watching as the man floated past, pulled roughly by the strength of the current. In the distance, a tiny boat rocked on the waves. If this was the Ferryman, he certainly wasn't blessed with an impressive craft. Evie shaded her eyes against the bleak light and squinted at the floating speck. He was headed to the other shore, perhaps just now ferrying another soul to the Underworld.

Around her, the keening of the lost souls trapped within the waters of the Styx rose and fell like a song in the distance, distorted by the wind. Pale hands broke the surface every now and then accompanied by a sad wail, which rose to a crescendo and then fell to silence. Only to begin again.

Endless. Futile.

Creatures desperate for release.

Evie's heart clenched each time the sounds grew louder. She gritted her teeth and fought her every instinct, reminding herself every second that the Seals were the most important thing, here and now. Nothing else mattered.

A voice spoke nearby. Familiar and endearing. Another trick?

Another shade testing her with Patrick's voice? Evie squeezed her eyes shut, refusing to turn around.

"It is me, my child. Do not be afraid." Patrick spoke from close behind her. She turned. Her heart knocked against her ribs. He was standing right in front of her, a benevolent smile across his face. He held out a hand and Evie reached for it. But she hesitated.

Was she walking right into danger? This could be another trick. But her heart called to her and she placed her hand within his. His fingers felt strange, soft but in a vague way, as if she touched him in a dream.

He was there, but not there.

"What's happening? Why are you here so quickly? I thought the dead would only come to the river when they are buried and ready for the crossing?" Evie's heart jumped into her throat. What had Marcellus done?

"Time moves slower in the Underworld, child. This is now the third day after my death and the second since my burial."

"You've been here for a whole day? Why have you not crossed over yet?"

"I am stuck on this side of the river, Evangeline." His words were soft and gentle.

"Why? What's wrong?"

"I do not have the payment for my passage." Patrick looked at Evie, a knowing smile on his endearing face.

Evie stilled with shock. She'd had the silver coins in her hand when she'd been distracted by the broken glass.

"Oh no. I'm so sorry. I was going to place them on your eyes...I'm sure I..." Evie patted her pockets and retrieved the two coins from her back pocket. She placed the coins in Patrick's open palm. "It's not too late, is it?"

"No, no. It's not too late. I just need the coins to pay my friend Charon."

Evie laughed. Trust Patrick to make friends with the man who ferries the dead across the Styx. "You have been busy, I see." Once the words were out, she remembered it was her own fault he was stuck on this side of the river longer than was necessary. "I'm really sorry. I shouldn't have forgotten the coins."

"It doesn't matter now, child. I have the payment for my passage. And you had good reason to forget."

"You know?"

Patrick nodded. His spirit would have lingered for a while in the room after his demise. He would have witnessed her most intimate moments of grief and strangely, she didn't feel uncomfortable or exposed. The memory of her discovery of his body brought Evie back to the cause of his death.

"It was Marcellus, wasn't it?" Evie asked as anger spurted out with the words.

Patrick smiled.

"How?"

"Does it matter now?" He turned and stared out over the water.

"Yes, it matters. Why do you think I'm here?" Evie touched his arm, turning his attention back to her.

"I'm not sure.... I'm a little fuzzy on the specifics."

"It's the Seals he's after."

"The Seals of Hades?" Patrick's attention was focused again. He seemed to be having trouble concentrating on the conversation.

"Why didn't you tell me what they were?" Evie regarded Patrick, her face filled with disappointment. He had not trusted her enough.

"I didn't mean to put you in harm's way. I wanted to—" Patrick said softly before she cut him off.

"We were in danger as soon as Marcellus began to send us on the new missions," she said, eyebrows curved in accusation.

He laid a comforting hand on her arm. She ached for his arms to enfold her in a bear-hug like he used to do when she was little. He'd tended her scrapes and taught her the intricacies of life. This was the last time she would ever have a conversation with him, the last time he would provide much-needed advice.

"If I'd known his intention was to find the Seals and take the throne of the Underworld, I would have done everything possible to stop him."

"Precisely my point. You would have gone barreling in without thinking. You think with your heart, Evangeline. You must now learn to use this." Patrick tapped Evie at her temple.

"I could have done with some guidance," Evie grumbled.

"Tell me how you got here," Patrick said, sadness deepening the creases at the corners of his eyes as he ignored her petulance.

"I found a Seal. So did Ling. After Marcellus raided our rooms, we suspected something was up. My next assignment, Renfru, was a high-level demon. I managed to persuade him to give me his Seal and he led me to Baa'ruk."

"The Demon Overlord?" Patrick's eyebrows rose.

Evie nodded. "Barry filled me in on the finer points of the twelve Seals. There was no way I could allow Marcellus to attain such a powerful position."

While they were talking, Charon had made his way back from the other side of the river. Up close the boat was no longer just a plain wooden craft, but a vessel large enough to hold fifty men seated five across. The oars, twice as long as Charon's height, were hitched along the edge of the boat. Charon moored the craft and waited in silence.

Patrick squeezed Evie's hand in a last farewell and moved silently to the boat. He handed a coin to Charon who twirled it between his fingers then bit down hard on the silver. Satisfied, he motioned for Patrick to climb on board.

"Why did you give him only one coin, Patrick?" Evie had noticed Patrick held onto the second coin.

"Charon requires payment of one coin only. The second is for the trip back. If you ever get to leave." Patrick smiled at Evie and winked. The coin glinted in his hand.

"Wait. I need to cross too."

Charon stared at Evie, then motioned for her to step aboard. One step into the craft and Evie knew it wouldn't work. The boat rocked, straining against her weight. Why would her weight be enough to tip over such a large vessel?

"I will return for you." Charon's voice came out flat and unemotional.

Evie looked at Patrick with raised eyebrows. "The dead weigh almost nothing, Evie. The living are still as solid here in Hades as they are Earth-side."

"I guess I'll wait then." She shrugged, hiding her disappointment behind a smile.

Charon tipped Evie a small bow and pushed off. The slow slap of the oars against the water brought tears to her eyes. Patrick faced his destination, firmly choosing his fate. Evie settled down to wait for the Ferryman.

Now alone, she was at the mercy of the cries of the dead calling for her help. Soon, Evie's eyes filled with tears, this time none were for Patrick. Her body tensed and muscles hardened so much they were almost cramping. Something brushed Evie's shoulder and she whirled around, her heart thumping against her breastbone.

A young boy, hair a tousled blond mat, looked up at her, resignation deepening the lines of his young face. Evie steeled herself, trying not to permit the child's earnest face to bend her will. His voice was faint and garbled, as if he spoke into a gusting wind which grabbed his words and flung them to the ether. He held his hand out, palms outstretched, begging her for something. She couldn't hear what he called out, what he pleaded for. She was eager to step away from those bleak gray eyes, and the outstretched hand, which she imagined would grasp at her any second.

Her heart thudded in her chest, driving her to free herself. Behind her, white and silver wings smacked the air, snapped into place and lifted her off the ground. Magic may not work within the realms of the Underworld, but Evie's wings were not magic, they were part of her, life and soul.

Evie flew to a large rock, safe from the shades who would traverse the waters of the Styx for eternity. Evie's grasp of classic Greek mythology was fairly good. These were the wraiths of the wicked and the cursed. The souls of those who died an unworthy death or who took their own lives. The gods were a jealous lot. They guarded the gift of life, punishing those who spurned such a precious boon by casting the souls of those unworthy to the waters of the River of the Dead.

But there were holes in the theories. And no mention of the Seals had ever been made, either in the textbooks or by the teachers. Charon's name had been tossed to the students, but no one was told how to pay the Ferryman without money, just that those without the coin were cursed to walk the shore for a hundred years.

Evie's satchel hung tight around her neck and torso. She ached to put it down but was too afraid of losing the precious seals. She was sure they'd now left a bunch of bruises on her hip. Patrick had paid Charon with one silver coin and kept the other with him. He'd joked about needing it for his return journey. Evie had first thought he wasn't making sense but now it was clear. A journey into Hades means two crossings, one into Hades, and one to return home provided you entered alive.

Two crossings meant two coins. Evie ripped the satchel open and felt for the three smaller disks she'd tucked into a small side pocket. She spread them on her lap and studied each one. There were one set and a single coin. The pair bore the engravings of a boat, oars on its face, and coins on the flip side. How had she not made the connection?

The lone coin, with the three faces, had engravings of loaves of bread on its back. Baffled, Evie slid the single coin back into the bag and held onto the coins meant for the Ferryman. Almost an eternity passed while Evie waited for Charon to slap his paddle into the black waters and surge against the rush of the waves to return. She watched the boat bob on the misty water. Time was a strange and fickle thing while one was stuck in the Underworld. Where minutes passed for Evie, hours probably sped by for the Warriors of Irin.

The slap of Charon's paddle on the water grew louder and Evie scrambled to her feet to jog down to the water's edge. He moved faster than she expected and was already mooring the lines when she got to the boat. Charon's face was still devoid of emotion. Evie kind of understood his lack of feeling. Anyone charged with ferrying the dead day-in, day-out would surely go berserk if they were affected by the cries of those he was unable to take across.

She climbed aboard, and again, the boat shivered. But this time it held, and Evie passed one of the coins to Charon. She waited as he studied the disk. Amazement and wonder shone from the face she'd thought unable to express any emotion.

"It is you?"

"I'm Evangeline, if that's what you mean." Evie was puzzled. Who was she supposed to be then?

She frowned and kept a close eye on the Ferryman as he set off across the water. Every few minutes, he would glance back at her, an odd smile on his lips, as if he knew a great secret and was bursting to tell someone. Evie chose to ignore him. Otherwise, she'd be shaking the man senseless until he confessed the secret.

The trip across the river seemed long as Evie had watched Charon's progress from the hill. In actuality it was interminable. It took close to an hour to reach the other shoreline. Evie was nodding off when the boat nudged the dock and Charon brushed past her to tie the mooring lines.

Evie rose on wooden legs and stumbled off the boat. As she

passed Charon, he grasped her hand and squeezed it between his own strong palms.

"Welcome to Erebus." He nodded and smiled a toothless grin, pumping her hand. "Go with the Gods."

Evie smiled back and nodded, backing away onto solid ground. Charon disappeared across the lake, evaporating into a strange mist that floated on the surface of the black water.

Evie looked around and sighed. So this was all real.

CHAPTER 16

The other shore was as different to the rocky barren land she'd come from as night was to day. Sand crunched beneath her bootheels. The path up to the trees was peppered with crushed seashells, then lined with long grass as it led deep into the trees, trees which were green and hung heavy with fruit, so succulent and ripe her mouth watered as she imagined the thick juices running down her chin as she sank her teeth into the soft flesh.

Evie jerked out of her reverie—the cawing of another errant raven stung her eardrums. She looked up and could only see a black fleck circling high up in the sky. Hard to comprehend they were beneath the Earth, deep within its bowels.

Baa'ruk's warning still rang hot in her ears. *Eat nothing, drink nothing.* So, no matter how tempting the fruit might be, no food of the Underworld would satiate the cravings now building within her.

She stared longingly at the heavily laden peach tree. Hunger gripped Evie's gut, and she recalled her last meal hours ago. Dragging her attention from the fruit, she sighed and checked her watch to confirm the time, then swallowed a gasp. Her watch had stopped at seven this morning as she'd crossed the threshold of the cave to begin her journey.

Now Evie began to worry. About how long she'd been down in the Underworld. Whether Baa'ruk was safe or if his boss had punished him by sending him back to the underworlds of Hell. If Marcellus had discovered his collection of Seals was gone.

Evie sighed, helpless despite her angelic nature. Usually she felt imbued with a power that made her stronger, faster, and smarter than the next Joe. Today, she felt far from the savior Nephilim.

Evie walked through a large orchard that ran along the shore in both directions as far as the eye could see. The trees were filled with shining fruit, varieties of every fruit available to mankind and some she'd never seen before. She passed strange and unusual creatures. A two-headed peacock wailed and honked as she passed.

Don't stop, don't dally.

Evie had no control of her legs. They seemingly took her where she needed to go. How did she really know where to go, which path to take, which ones to avoid?

Forward was good.

At last, she came to a clearing, Grass padded the ground, thick and green. It opened out onto the mouth of another cave so like the one she'd taken to arrive here that she felt slightly dizzy with déjà vu. Her steps faltered as she approached the dark maw of the cave and Evie wished she were back home, far from these deadly dilemmas.

Water trickled from the walls of the damp, cool cave as if the rocks were alive and perspiring with the effort of keeping the tunnel open so she could pass. Evie entered the tunnel and made her way deeper inside. Soon she felt as if she were walking for miles in the semi-darkness when she suddenly reached the end.

The tunnel opened into a large cave and Evie turned slowly on her heel to study the five entrances which now lay before her.

The hairs on the back of her neck stood on end seconds before a roar reverberated through the tunnel, rippling the sand on the floor and sending showers of rock-dust to the ground and onto Evie's bare head. She tensed for the collapse of the tunnel or for something large and dangerous to fall onto her head.

When nothing happened, she relaxed and strained to discover the origin of the howling bellow. Another roar and the offending tunnel was clearly identified as it shook with the sound. Slivers of shale fell to the ground, striking the stone floor and shattering into fine shards.

Evie entered the cave and walked on tiptoe toward the sound. Intermittent and irregular, the next howls made Evie pause often to allow her to track the cry through the darkness. The tunnel ended, and Evie came face-to-face with a hideously strange creature.

Cerberus. *The* Cerberus.

He pawed the ground at Evie's feet and stared at her with each of his three grotesque heads. His roar chilled the bones down Evie's spine. Confronted by a creature which thus far had only existed in myth, she was ready to choose flight if it came to it. The dog was larger than anything she could have imagined. Much larger. The top of Evie's head barely reached his shoulder and she had to crane her neck to get the full view of his dripping jaws.

Despite the cool air flowing through the chamber, eau-de-wet-dog hung in the cavern and coated her throat as she breathed. That, combined with the fetid stench of Cerberus' bad breath, and Evie was ready to hurl. Now she was looking at her empty stomach with a more positive note.

Evie was partly grateful that the animal was tied, tethered by a chain with links as large as her wrists. The problem was the length of the chain gave the creature the run of the small cave, ensuring nobody could pass without becoming Cerberus chow.

He roared again. Or was it they? Evie was confused as the

cacophony of three simultaneous howls slowly died down. He tugged at the chain, veins turgid at his neck, bulging. Was it possible for a mythical creature to burst a blood vessel?

It may have been the sound of the blood rushing from Evie's over active heart, but all three heads turned to her at the same time. Six eyes examined her head to foot followed by another bone-quivering roar. Each head faced Evie, jowls open, saliva dripping in great globs to one common set of paws. Their teeth sent shudders of fear through her body. Three sets of vicious canines glinted at her.

Cerberus rushed at her, and even though Evie knew he was tied, she still screamed and stumbled backward, landing on her rear with a thud. Her feet were two inches from him and she watched in a complex mix of amusement and fear as the three heads fought for the chance to sniff at her boots.

Evie plucked her foot away from the searching muzzles and jumped up.

Now what?

"You are wasting your time, little one."

The rough, deep voice was so unexpected, Evie jumped with shock. She turned around and faced the speaker who was currently lounging against the rough wall, uncaring that the moisture seeped into the soft silk of his shirt. Arms crossed and foot supporting himself on the rock behind him, the stranger shook his head. His dark curly hair moved around his shoulders like a mane of a lion.

"Well, I have to pass him." Evie spoke, wondering if he was an apparition or another shade. She was sure she hadn't been followed when she left the river's edge.

"As I said, you really don't have much of a chance."

"Can you explain what you mean by that?" Evie felt her face heat up in anger, sure there were two bright spots on her cheek-bones revealing her annoyance. Who was this mysterious naysayer? And where did he come from? More than ever, Evie wished for guidance. But Patrick was dead, probably completing his journey as she stood shivering in her boots. As for Baa'ruk, he wasn't even allowed to be here. "And who exactly are you?"

"You won't have much chance getting past the terrible trio here. They will eat you alive. Besides, many better travelers have come this far and turned back."

His arrogance spiked Evie's annoyance. "How would you know?"

"Because I have been around a good long while. Long enough to know that only the deserving get to pass Cerberus." The stranger grinned, pleased to have stumped Evie.

"I'm here to see Hades. I have to get past." She was losing her patience with his cocky arrogance.

"Oh, you have an appointment to see His Highness?" He curved an eyebrow.

"No. But it's important," she assured him, but immediately felt deflated on seeing his grin widen.

"That's what they all say. And that's why you need to get Cerberus to let you pass. Which is not going to happen."

Evie ignored his jibe and turned on him, asking, "Who are you?"

"Oh, I don't think we've met before, but Ares is the name." There was a ringing in Evie's ears, accompanied but the sudden intense need to faint. Ares was the bloody God of War. "Nothing to say?" Ares smiled, apparently enjoying Evie's discomfort.

"Why do you care if I pass or not?" He was beginning to get on her nerves, God of War or not.

"It's the blood, you see. I am drawn to this place. I quite enjoy the way Cerberus rips his victims apart. It's especially fun to see the three of them fight for the good parts." Ares grinned and Evie wasn't certain he was kidding. His eyes were devoid of emotion as he spoke, uncaring of the agony of the creature's victims.

"And you think he's going to eat me?" she asked, her voice dry.

"Oh, I'm certain of it." Cocky, arrogant and provocative.

Perhaps he got away with it because of his looks, but Evie was not entranced by this god.

Ares' confidence unsettled Evie. Made her jittery and uncertain that she would actually get past the creature. The huge hulking dog paced before her, turning around twice before coming back to look straight at her. The three heads each looked in a different direction, and for an instant, their position brought to mind the lone coin.

Evie slipped her hand into the satchel at her side, out of Ares' line of sight, and withdrew the gleaming disk inscribed with the three heads. She hadn't immediately made the link because the heads on the coin were human, but there were loaves of bread inscribed on the back. If Evie recalled the myths properly, then it was food she needed to get past the beast.

She was stumped. With three heads, which one would she give the coin to? Cowardice won out and she placed the coin on the floor and kicked it toward Cerberus. Let the three fight over who grabs up the coin.

Meanwhile, Ares craned his neck to get a better look at the coin.

"Where did you get that?" Shock and anger simmered in his voice. "Who gave you that?"

"Nobody gave it to me. I found it." Evie backed away from the infuriated god. She'd never had a conversation with a deity before and speaking with one whose fury alone was potentially lethal, Evie silently begged for divine assistance. A few seconds later when no help arrived, she cast a quick glance at the dog. The middle head had grasped the coin within its teeth and tossed its head side to side. The other two nudged him, each trying and failing to get him to release it.

At last it fell to the stone floor with a clang, which echoed all the way along the tunnels and came back again, hauntingly beautiful. But the reverberations did not stop. Cerberus moved to hover over the now glowing disk.

"Told you it won't be that easy." Ares chuckled behind Evie, clearly enjoying her initial failure.

"What now?" she snapped.

"Be nice, or I won't help you." Evie wanted ask him how his sneering would be helping her but she clamped her mouth shut. "You have to answer a question."

She raised her eyebrows, waiting.

"Cerberus had three heads. What purpose do they serve?"

"What do you mean?"

"Are you slow or something?" Ares asked, his voice slick with ice as he pushed off the wall and drew closer. "What do each of Cerberus' three heads represent?"

Evie scanned the panting dog, who now lay on all fours, staring at the shimmering disk with longing. Long strings of drool dripped from all three jaws and all three pink tongues. Each head was identical to the next.

Evie paused before the disk, afraid to pick it up, but knowing she should have a good look at it. Maybe it held a clue. The side facing upward was the one engraved with the loaves of bread. She tried to picture the engraving on the other side. Three human heads. Evie recalled that she'd been initially confused as the heads were human, but the coin was for the three-headed dog.

She pictured the heads, one facing left, one forward and the last one facing right. *What would that mean? Hades looking three different ways. Four directions. Four seasons.* She recalled a trick question about the seasons of a man's life, but that didn't apply. Day and night were two.

Evie strained to recall anything that Patrick may have told her for clues. Patrick had so loved learning. Had always maintained that people could learn so much from the past because the past shaped the future.

Evie stiffened. *The past and the future.*

That was it.

She turned to Ares. "Past, present and future?"

Ares stared, aghast and slowly turning pink. Evie hoped it wasn't anger.

"Close, but no cigar!"

"What do you mean? What else is there?" Evie was flabbergasted.

"The answer must be exactly as it is meant to be spoken. Only then will Cerberus be tamed to your hand and allow you to pass." Ares' smile was triumphant, as if he knew it was impossible for her to get the answer right. As far as Evie knew there were only a few ways to say past, present and future.

"What has been, what is, and what shall be?" Evie took a chance, hoping she was right. She had no other options left.

Ares' face turned bright red as Cerberus's chains began clinking. Evie turned to see the dog walking to her, dragging the long chain behind him. When he reached her, he nudged her hip with the nearest head, urging her to walk toward the other side of the cavern.

Ares, the epitome of the angry god, lashed out, charging at Evie with an angry roar. Cerberus turned and head-butted the god just as he reached her. The God of War lost the battle as his head bounced against the rock wall and he slumped unconscious to the floor.

Evie walked on, moving only because Cerberus was pushing at her back. But she continued to look over her shoulder every so often, not sure whether she was concerned Ares would revive and chase after her or if she was worried that he may be dead. Only when she lost sight of him was she able to think about her mission. She just hoped coming to Hades wasn't a huge mistake.

CHAPTER 17

$\mathcal{E}$vie walked with Cerberus, who trotted alongside her, his great haunches bumping against her shoulders. The dog's three heads repeatedly turned to look behind him. Was he keeping an eye—or six—out for Ares? Thankfully, there was no sound from the unconscious god. Hopefully he wouldn't be there on her way out. She hitched the satchel around her, feeling its comforting weight against her hip.

She'd used two disks so far, and she'd need to keep the remaining coin for Charon on her trip home. That left her with eight of the actual Seals. She hoped Hades would be happy to receive this gift. Hoped too that he would find a better place to hide the Seals. Whoever thought of charging a bunch of demons with the job of guarding the Ascension Seals needed to get their head checked.

The dog led Evie deeper into the warren of caves. Water leaked from the stone as if crying for Evie on her journey. The tunnel was marked every so often by a small stream of water which ran across the floor and Evie had to keep a close eye on the ground to ensure she didn't wade into a crossing stream.

Cerberus was happy enough and stopped regularly to lap at a trickle of water with one or all of his pink tongues.

At last, the passage opened out onto another large cavern and Cerberus stopped. When she turned to the dog, he whined, the sound coming simultaneously from each of the three throats. The creature barked at Evie, spraying globs of saliva onto her. Evie hid her head behind her arms.

As Cerberus turned and loped off into the darkness of the passage, his tail swung around and hit Evie full on the side of her head. So hard was the blow that she lost her balance and ended up on her rear for the second time since she entered these tunnels.

Cerberus pounded through the tunnel. Evie could hear his paws slamming the ground as he returned to his post to guard the entrance to the Underworld.

Evie stood in the huge cavern where the ceiling was so high she could barely see it in the darkness pooled above. A number of tunnels led off the open space. How would she know which tunnel to follow? The Seals held no clues.

A cool breeze blew, snaking through the maze of tunnels. Evie shivered. When would she see the sun again? The last time she'd felt the warm rays of the sun on her skin was that morning as she ate stale beignets with a blond, dreadlocked albino demon.

Now, standing around would do no good. She had to make a decision—which way to go? One of the tunnels beckoned, wider, larger and brighter than the rest. If it looked welcoming, it might just be so. She walked down the tunnel, following its meandering path.

There had been other tunnels to choose from, but all of the other gaping holes in the rock were cold and uninviting. Her footsteps were dulled by a fine layer of black moss which clung to the stone beneath her feet like a luxurious carpet.

As she travelled farther along the passageway, various tokens of comfort began to appear. Small, elegant metal torches were fixed to the walls, throwing soft, yellow light into the passage. The walls were straighter, drier, and smoother—less cave-like than the rest of the tunnels throughout her journey.

Her travels were taking her deeper and deeper into the bowels of the Earth, and Evie felt the ground drop as the tunnel sloped slightly.

Evie reached a doorway sealed off by a solid stone door. The lintel towered above her, almost twice her height. Great hinges on the door, thick as her arms, were constructed of solid black metal. Evie's fingers lingered on the rough metal.

A doorknob as large as her fist sat in the middle of the door right in front of her nose. She laid her palm on the stone. Through the thickness of the stone, Evie felt a pulsing, like a heart throbbing softly within the door. Or behind it.

Evie tried to turn the knob, tugging and pulling to no avail. Angry and tired, she pushed, the door hard. The shove was all the door needed as it swung open, so smooth and quiet Evie barely took notice.

Her eyes were fixed on a table at the center of the room. It sat there, large and heavy and seemingly cold. But Evie felt drawn to it. Some power throbbed within the stone. Her ears felt it pulsating; her heart beat in tandem with it.

Before she knew it, she was beside the table. When her fingers touched the surface, Evie pulled back, startled. How she got there she did not know. It seemed to have a strange power over her, so strong she was unable to control her own body.

The room was cold, stone walls and floor. Nothing adorned any of the room's surfaces.

The table took pride of place. At each of the eight corners of the octagonal table, a circular depression was carved into the stone. Evie walked around the table, touching the hollows, feeling the stone, entranced. As she took the last corner to complete the circuit, her satchel knocked the stone corner and the Seals began to sing.

The sweet sound of the Seals rang around the room, each ring echoing into each other as it bounced against the walls. A hundred bells clanged with haunting beauty and Evie's entire body sang with it. Her back tingled and her wings burgeoned, pressing against flesh and bone to answer the magical call, but she tamped back the urge to release them.

She tugged the strap of the satchel over her head and laid it on the table. Opening the flap, she was greeted by an extraordinary sight. Evie stood in slack-jawed awe staring at the Seals inside it.

All eight Seals lay free of their wrappings. Each Seal glowed golden while it sang with its sisters. Scripts once engraved upon each Seal's surface now swirled around as if alive as black, indecipherable words danced on the edges of the disks. The eight Seal engravings spun clockwise inside the swirling script. At the center of the disks, a single symbol now stood out, glowing with a yellow intensity, which burned against the back of Evie's eyes.

Evie's heart jumped with shock.

Nine mini-Seals engraved upon each Seal. But after retrieving the Seals from Marcellus' hiding-place they'd ended up with eight Seals and three large coins. Although she was still amped with the energy of the table and the Seal-Song combined, Evie's heart was heavy with disappointment. In desperation, Evie emptied the Seals onto the stone table and spread them out, counting as she went.

Eight, still only eight.

What did you think? That counting would make eight into nine?

The next instant, a force stronger than all her Nephilim power buffeted Evie. The shockwave was so strong she staggered backward, struggling to stay on her feet. Just as suddenly, the force of the power reversed and began to pull Evie toward the table.

Out of her line of sight, the Seals were skimming the surface of the table, swirling around the table as if they had a mind of their own. The Seals found individual little homes for themselves at the depressions at the eight corners. The Seals spun within the cells as if excited to be home. Evie's ears hummed and breathing was becoming a problem.

The mysterious force tugged and pulled at her, insistent, unbreakable. Evie's progress was halted sharply as she slid, spread-eagled over the edge of the table. Her belt buckle caught at the lip at the edge of the table, straining against the magnetic pull.

Just when she suspected there was a chance to break out of this demonic control, the metal of the buckle bent abruptly and Evie slid forward. She grasped at the smooth rock, scrabbling to dig her fingers into anything that might halt her progress.

Evie was too shocked to scream. She watched as blood from her broken fingernails smeared the table. Invisible hands jerked her upward and she found herself flat on her back, hovering a foot above the table. She flailed in the air. Her wings pushed for freedom, and though she wanted to release them, she was unable to summon them.

There was no time to be afraid.

Evie turned her head, eager to find a way out. The Seals sang their haunting lullaby, glowing golden and spinning clockwise. Light flowed like a beacon from each seal, shooting to the stone ceiling. They still sang, louder, more beautiful, more haunting than ever.

The sound penetrated the haze, which encased Evie like a silken cocoon. The music enchanted her. The sound of heavenly song. A slow vibration tapped at her breast, slowly increasing speed until it knocked crazily against her sternum. It sang through her bones and her blood, ramming her chest in a tattoo.

Evie, alarmed at the rapid succession of the pounding on her chest, craned her neck to see what was stomping on her breast-bone like a shaman doing a war dance. The leather thong around her neck was pulled taut, rubbing her neck raw. At the end of the thong, her medallion jumped in a wild frenzy.

The medallion was a gift from her father, Gabriel. He left the pendant with Patrick for safekeeping until she'd reached her Turn—the time when a Nephilim embraces either the human or angel side. Evie kept the medallion close to her—much like she kept the memory of her father.

Gabriel had entrusted Evie to Patrick's care when she was an infant. And though she understood his reasons, there were times when she wallowed in self-pity at her abandonment. Now she feared the very thing which held her to her father.

The medallion rose above Evie until the thong pulled hard on her neck. Evie desperately tilted her head forward, hoping to give it a chance to slip off her neck. The thong was pulled off her head, lifting her hair with it as it was sent spinning upward. It hovered just out of her reach.

Evie was spellbound as streams of light from each of the eight Seals began to bend and move toward the medallion. At last, all eight questing rays of light joined, forming a conical cage around Evie.

Now the Nephilim was very afraid.

Evie's wings pushed against her back, so painful she felt faint. Cool stone touched her back with a small thump. She was now lying on the table. The word altar may be more appropriate as she felt very much like a living sacrifice.

A flash of white light and energy passed through Evie's body and blackness claimed her.

CHAPTER 18

Julian looked up from the book lying open on his lap, certain some strange sound had penetrated his concentration. There weren't many things able to distract him from a reading of Horace.

There, he heard it again. The ringing of a bell, so sweet and delicate it could easily be mistaken for the light, airy song of a lyre. He sat upright and closed the book. He did not need to mark his page, as he knew exactly where he was in his reading. In fact, he knew the text by heart, having read it repeatedly for two thousand years.

Julian swung open the door to his living area and tilted his head, keen to pinpoint the origin of the sound. The chimes rang through the walls of rock, up the soles of his feet. Most distracting. He followed the tunnel toward the Hall of Judgment, forced to hazard a guess as to the direction.

Perhaps Persephone had arranged some entertainment in another attempt at winning his affections. Julian shook his head. When would she realize he had zero affection for her? That she had zero hope of gaining even one iota of his affection no matter what foolish attempt she made? He may have succeeded Hades in his role, but it certainly didn't mean he had to take Persephone as a wife.

A frown marred his strong forehead as he followed the sound in the direction of the Ascension Hall. He began to compare the sound he heard reverberating around him now to the sound of the Seals on that day, two millennia ago, when Hades, God of the Underworld, had chosen a lucky young Roman as his replacement.

Temporary, he'd said. Because he needed time to think, he'd said.

Now, two thousand years later, one would think Hades would have had enough of his thinking. But the sounds of those Seals certainly didn't herald Hades' return. Julian was sure it meant something entirely worse than the old king returning to take back his throne. Because the Seals did not make a god into a king.

They made a human into a god.

When he reached the huge stone door, Julian stopped in his tracks. The door was shut, as tight as it had always been. But a weak light shone from the gaps around the edges, as if even the beveled edges of the door had no power to stop the light from bending on its way out of the room.

He grasped the knob and pushed the door with all his might, putting his shoulder into it. It swung open, slowly and silently. The room was the source of the ringing. Lilting chimes bounced back and forth against the hard stone walls, filling the room with music.

Julian gasped, horrified. The hair on his body stood on end. Yes, the Seals had called him. And coming here, following the sound, had been a very, very bad idea. A girl lay prone and still upon the Ascension Table. A very beautiful girl surrounded by a golden, angelic glow. For the briefest second, Julian saw a pair of magnificent white and silver wings spread out beneath her, as she lay entranced by the Magic of the Seals. Julian blinked and the vision of the wings disappeared. He must have imagined it.

The magic held the girl within a pyramid of eight streams of light and Julian wondered if it had looked like this when he received the throne of Hades. He had been just as unconscious as *this* girl, oblivious to his surroundings, as his entire life was wiped away and a new, never-ending existence was thrust upon him against his will.

Now it was her turn.

EVIE SENSED a presence in the room. She remained frozen on the table, unable to move her head to see who had entered. The dreaded sense of being so vulnerable surged through her limbs. Fresh air skimmed her body and she registered its light touch in spite of the hold which the Seals and their music had on her. The single medallion hovered above her hung like an all-seeing eye.

Her medallion, which had lain against her heart for so many years. Evie felt the slight tug of betrayal on her soul. Did Gabriel know what it was that he'd left for her? And did he know the danger he'd put her in?

Evie would have shuddered with anger if she had been able to move. She hoped she was wrong, hoped Gabriel had not been aware of how important the relic was.

Evie blinked and felt the moisture in the hair above her ears. She had shed her first tears. The medallion had been an object loved and treasured for so long. Now, as she had no choice but to stare at it, she acknowledged that all along it had possessed a purpose beyond her tiny existence. The medallion was octagonal like the stone table. Each point held a small circle clearly meant to hold the stream of light which now passed through it. All eight beacons met above the medallion in one shimmering cone of glowing white.

Her medallion seemed to be acting as the key to this entire— what was she supposed to call this whole thing anyway? Evie wasn't sure at all what had just happened. Perhaps it had a whole lot more to do with the Seals than it did with her. She hoped it did.

She tried to remain calm, but it was a tiny bit difficult since she was trapped in this invisible pool of energy. That was a terrifying thought. With the luxury of her angelic blood gifting her with an indefinite lifespan, Evie had never before contemplated her death.

The thought of meeting a permanent end thrust a sharp knife of pain into her gut. She still had so many things to do before she met her maker. There was Gabriel. And saving the Irin from Marcellus.

And finding Hades to return his Seals.

Of course, Hades might not be a very happy dude once he found out about this whole Seal-singing light display.

Evie struggled to move her head but—nothing. She had to know who had entered the room. What did they want? Fear coursed through her veins. She was unable to move, and a total stranger stood there with her.

A sudden surge of energy caught Evie's attention as the Seals ceased their song in one burst of dead silence. The air grew heavy, dense, pressing on her lungs. Even the thin strobes of light which shone from each Seal fell back into itself like a fountain of white waves.

As suddenly as the chimes fell into silence, so did they spring to life again, more urgent, this time. Out of each Seal rose a dark mass that resembled the Seal itself. Each splotch of black rose, spinning and swirling on its journey toward Evie. She stiffened. The destination of the eight spinning splotches was *her*.

She struggled against the invisible field that still held her prisoner. As they floated to her, they grew darker and more defined and Evie recognized them as the script engraved on the rim of each Seal. The crazy spinning increased, until Evie began to feel queasy just looking at them.

They swirled around her body, hovering as if uncertain of their final destination. At last, they pooled around her right arm, lowering slowly while still spinning in an almost uncontrollable dance. Just when they got to within an inch of Evie's arm, all eight oscillating dark orbs disappeared. Evie sighed, relieved and hoping that was the last she would see of them. But as she relaxed, sharp, agonizing, burning pain shafted through her forearm, so full and intense it struck her right to the bone.

Dear God, let the pain end.

And when it didn't, Evie went to grasp the edge of her leather jacket to pull it off her before she realized she could move. A deep sense of foreboding enveloped her. The burning and the absence of the Seals' song didn't mean anything good. Finally, she was able to move. She tore the jacket off and she rolled up the sleeve of her shirt.

Evie couldn't breathe when she saw her forearm. In spite of the agony blistering her skin, the sight of the angelic script engraved into her very skin filled her with a deep sense of peace and tranquility.

Until she saw who'd entered the room.

She needn't have feared his presence. One look at his face and it was clear he meant her no harm. But the look in his eyes made her stomach twist. He held his forearm in exactly the same place Evie now felt the strange burn biting into her skin.

She watched him, entranced by the strangely compelling expression on his face and his odd movements. He rolled up his sleeve, the cream silk folding over softly, to reveal his own strong, muscular marked forearm.

His markings were faint lines of scars rather than a tattoo, while hers were dark and prominent.

CHAPTER 19

Julian stared at his forearm, shocked, worried and terrified. Who was this girl and what had she just done?

The Marks of Hades which had been emblazoned upon his skin for the last two millennia had faded. Much more like an old tattoo rather than the deep, dark angelic script he'd been so used to seeing for all these years. Julian's eyes were drawn to the girl's own slim, almost fragile forearm where thick, black scrawls swirled and curved around her pale skin. The pain, creasing the corners of her eyes and washing out the color from her skin, confirmed his greatest fear.

The mantle of the Ruler of the Underworld had just been passed to this young girl. A girl whose eyes seemed to call to him, whose pain made him want to reach out and caress her cheek, to promise her it would soon get better.

"Who are you? What are you doing here?" Julian's voice shook. He was unsure which was stronger—his anger, his attraction or his fear. How would a mere girl survive the turmoil of the living hell he had undergone for so many centuries? And, even worse, how would he be able to adjust to a mortal life now? After all these centuries? Would he soon shrivel up and die? Would he not soon turn into a pile of dust?

The girl sat on the cold stone. Despite the strength and courage in her face, her slim arms quivered. She didn't answer his question. Just sat there dazed, in shock. Julian closed the distance between them and stood in front of her until she was forced to lift her face and look at him.

When she did, he was mesmerized. Even from within the depths of his confusion and fear, Julian felt himself caught up in something much bigger and stronger than he was. A whirlpool of emotions that he'd sworn had died hundreds of years before swirled within him.

Her eyes were a clear, bright blue like the sea on a sun-drenched day. Her hair fell from its tie, thick and black and luxurious. Although fear filled those eyes, he also recognized strength and confusion. She felt very much the same as he did.

"How did you get here?" This time his tone was softer, thinking more about her feelings than his own potential mortality.

"I came to find Hades." She cast her eyes about as if she still searched for him.

"What do you want with him?" Julian's eyes narrowed. This was not a common occurrence. Hades had not had a guest in what...forever now?

"I had to give him something... but..." She hesitated and looked at the stone table, brow furrowed. "But...I think I may be too late."

"So what was it you were bringing m—him?" Julian stumbled on the words, wanting to eke out a bit more information before he confirmed his identity.

"His damned Seals. Now look at the mess those damned things have gotten me into." She waved her hand at the Seals, which lay quiet and innocent in each corner of the octagonal table. She looked down at her arm and her lips quivered.

Julian feared she would cry, and having no idea what he would do with a crying woman, he said quickly, "Who are you?"

"My name is Evangeline. I work for…someone who wants the Seals for himself. I thought it was better to bring them here rather than let an evil man take possession of them. I think they are powerful." She looked up at Julian and swung her feet around to jump off the table. "Can you help me find him?"

She swayed on her feet and then winced as she caught the edge of the table with her tattooed arm. Julian understood her pain. Remembered the agony from when he'd first received the marks. And admired her strength. For a girl, she endured the burning quite courageously.

"So, can you take me to him? Hades?" She stood almost as tall as Julian, and waited for his answer.

"Er, that's easier than you may think."

"Why is that?"

"Because, my dear, *you* are Hades."

"ARE YOU INSANE?" Evie stared at him, unable to accept his words. He must be a bit soft in the head, albeit super hot. Maybe lack of sunshine's been affecting his brain cells?

"Not really. In fact, I believe I am quite sane." His smile was calm, almost serene. Too serene.

"Certainly does not seem that way to me. Now can you find this Hades dude and tell him I need to speak to him?"

"I told you who Hades was, but since you won't believe me, maybe you can explain how you came to be in possession of the Seals? They were supposed to be hidden away a thousand years ago." He didn't move, just folded his arms and waited for her to respond.

Evie narrowed her eyes. He was all sexy, hard strength that called wildly to something deep inside her. Honey blond hair with pale streaks so incongruous on someone who lived in the dark holes of the earth.

Perhaps he was not from around here? Muscles where he needed them and none where he didn't. His biceps bulged beneath the soft silk of his sleeves. Strong chin, keen eyes, aristocratic Roman nose. Evie's pulse raced. She liked what she saw far too much.

"How come you know so much about where Hades hid the Seals?"

"Because he told me himself," he answered, the smile disappearing from his lips, the hard lines on his face making him appear much older.

"So where is he?"

"I'm afraid I have no idea. He said he needed time to think. But he has been gone for two millennia. And I haven't even received a postcard." A hint of sadness touched his eyes as he spoke. Perhaps he was a friend of Hades? This whole idea was preposterous. Hades gone for two thousand years?

"So who's been looking after the place since he's been gone?" Evie stared him down, daring him to hold back. She had questions he would not be able to avoid.

He sighed then. "I have."

"Huh? You?" Evie swallowed hard.

"Yes. That's what I have been trying to tell you. I was the last Ruler of the Underworld. Chosen by Hades."

"What do you mean the last ruler?" Evie felt like she was one of those dumb, vacuous girls who only ever thought about guys and the size of their boobs.

"*You* are the new Ruler. That"—he pointed at the table, now silent and still as if nothing strange had just happened—"what just happened…that made you the new Hades."

Evie, for once, was unable to find anything to say. She'd brought the Seals here to return them to Hades. The last thing she'd wanted was to be transformed into the new Ruler of the Underworld.

"No, no, no, no, no." She laughed, uncertain and a bit scared as she shook her head vehemently. He had to be kidding. "That's not possible. No. This is some kind of sick joke, right?"

"I don't joke. The Seals chose you and made you the next ruler. Which means *I* am now mortal." Evie did a double take.

Words expressed with an odd mixture of relief and fear.

"Mortal?" Evie recalled his words a few minutes before. "Right, Hades chose you, so you were mortal...two thousand years ago?"

"That is right. Well deduced. You have quite a scholarly mind, Evangeline."

"Yeah," she said.

Being around a thousand years will do that to a girl.

CHAPTER 20

The silence in the room was a stark and painful contrast to the humming ringing which had so recently pierced Evie's ears.

"Come, there is nothing left to do here." He had a hand to her back, gently guiding her out of the room. His palm seared her skin as heat sizzled through her, making her knees weak. Evie swallowed hard, trying to tamp down her traitorous heartbeat.

She really needed to keep her mind on her current catastrophe. Evie looked back at the Seals sunk so deep and solid into the stone she was fairly certain there was not much beyond total destruction that could remove them.

For now, they were safe.

Metal bit into her hands and she looked down to see the medallion in her palm. She must have grabbed it at some point, though she could not remember doing anything remotely as energetic as that. She slid it into her jacket pocket and blinked back tears.

Red hot sparks of panic threatened to erupt into full-blown hysteria. Not a common reaction for an Irin Warrior. *Patrick would be proud.* Evie breathed, then made a tight fist and tried to channel her hysteria.

Didn't work.

"No. You have to do something. Can't you change it?"

She looked at his hard profile as they walked, not slowing a single step. He walked with a lethal grace that made Evie's mouth suddenly dry. She shook her head. What was the matter with her?

She forced herself to pay attention to his words. "Not until twenty-eight days have passed."

"You mean I have a whole month to enjoy this?"

Evie thrust her arm out at Julian, almost punching him in the ribs. He avoided the blow and placed a hand on her arm, which she shrugged off far too quickly. And although she wanted to ignore it, she could not deny that it was the simmering heat where his flesh touched hers that set her on edge.

Off balance.

"Don't touch me. I don't even know who you are." He removed his hand and Evie suddenly felt bereft. She gritted her teeth. She really needed to get a hold of herself. She was going to be stuck here with him for a month after all.

Evie stiffened. Twenty-eight Hades days meant about three months of earth days. Too long. Who knew what havoc Marcellus would wreak in that time. But right now, there was nothing she could do about it.

"My name is Julian Tiberius," Julian said, giving her a low bow and bringing her attention back to him.

"Tiberius, like Emperor Tiberius?"

Julian shrugged. "Common enough name."

"Okay, Julian, so what am I supposed to do here for the next month?" She scanned the passage as they began to walk. "It's not as if you need a re-decorator. Pretty snazzy place for the Underworld."

She'd made a decision before he had spoken his first word. Somewhere between his first shocked look and their exit of the cursed room, Evie had decided not to reveal her true Immortal Nephilim nature. Whether it was instinct or survival, it seemed best to keep it under wraps for as long as possible. If she could go home without revealing that particular tidbit, she would be quite satisfied.

"I've been down here for a long time. One needs to live with a few comforts to make life worthwhile."

Julian guided Evie into another room, larger and airier than the previous one. A lot more comfortable too. The room was littered with sofas, tables and bookshelves filled to the brim with books of every age, shape, and size. A warmth and personality drew Evie into the room, whispering of comfort and relaxation and peace.

Evie looked around in silence, trying to understand the position Julian had been in. She sat on the nearest couch, not sure what to do with her hands so she folded them in her lap. Her forearm still stung, but the pain no longer pierced her as deeply as before. She'd tugged her sleeve over it and now left it covered, still a bit afraid to see the black script which confirmed that all of this was not a dream.

"Haven't you been lonely?" Then Evie remembered Hades' consort, feeling a cold stab of jealousy spike through her. Then she asked hopefully, "Hey, did Hades take Persephone with him on his travels?"

Evie twisted in her seat to watch Julian as he poured her a drink. The sight of the drink made her aware that her throat was parched, and her body was screaming for rest. The sight of his hands, fingers long and elegant, made her stomach twist uncomfortably.

"No. He left her here in my care. She hasn't been too happy about that." Julian spoke softly, eyes far away as if contemplating that relationship.

"I take it Persephone hasn't made you feel welcome?" Evie arched an eyebrow, trying to remain impartial.

"Oh, she's made me feel welcome." Julian smiled uncomfortably. "Perhaps a little too welcome."

"Mmhh, she got the hots for you?" Evie asked, smiling as twin spots of heat touched his cheeks. Then she chastised herself. What was wrong with her? How dare she be so familiar with the Ruler of the Underworld?

Julian continued, unaware of Evie's sudden discomfort. "Something like that. I guess she's lonely without him."

"You like her?" Somehow the thought of Julian in love with Persephone made Evie feel slightly ill.

"No. I believe *that* has been a problem for her." He gave a wry smile.

"Ooh, won't take no for answer?" When he shook his head, she said, "Where I come from that's call sexual harassment."

Julian laughed. "I know about your sexual harassment, and yes, it probably fits. But I do feel sorry for her. Being deserted by one's husband is probably not an easy thing to get used to. I have tried to help her. But I don't think I've done the right things."

"What's wrong with saying no?" Evie had to force herself to calm her rapid heartbeat.

What was the matter with her? She just couldn't keep her stupid mouth shut. She wanted to tear out Persephone's eyes for even looking at Julian. But this man-god was nobody to her.

"Maybe when you say it over and over again for two thousand years?" Julian smiled ruefully as he handed Evie a glass filled with a lemon drink, complete with muddled mint and a slice of lemon for garnish. Nice.

Their fingers touched, and her skin absorbed the virile heat of his as fire sparked and raced up her arm. She cleared her throat. "Well then, there you have it. She should have given up after about...oh...two hundred years?" Evie smiled as serenely as she could.

He sat across from her and asked, "There is something I need to know about the Seals. There were eight Seals hidden Earth-side. How did you find the ninth Seal?"

"I didn't find it." He stared at her, his brow furrowed in confusion. "I had it with me all along." Evie frowned. She felt the weight of the medallion in her pocket, but she didn't care so much about it now, in spite of it being a gift from Gabriel. That gift had turned out to be not so good, after all.

"Had it with you?" Julian stared at Evie, perplexed.

"My father gave it to my caregiver. He kept it for me until I came of age. I've had it with me for most of my life." Evie considered revealing to Julian how old she really was and immediately quashed the thought. Bad idea.

"Strange. It doesn't seem to be likely that the main Seal would be in the possession of a human."

"Are you saying I'm lying?" Evie was incensed, and yet it wasn't lost on her that she wasn't actually human, so she managed to calm down a little.

"No. No, I'm not. It's just that all the Seals should have been left in the care of a non-human."

"*That* I did find out." Evie nodded. "All the Seals were left in the care of demons."

"How did *you* end up with the Seals?"

Evie related the tale to Julian, leaving out any Nephilim-related information as well as not mentioning exactly who she worked for. What would she tell him if he asked? Evie decided to contend with that issue when the time came.

"That is an incredible story. And before you get upset, I do believe you."

Evie shut her mouth on the question she was about to ask him and smiled.

Just then the door swung open and a furiously beautiful woman entered the room.

Persephone.

"What is going on here?" Persephone fairly shook with fury.

Glowing blond ringlets fell to her waist. Topaz eyes glittered, and unblemished white cheeks glowed with violent anger. Evie stared at this fiery ball of fury and wondered if Julian knew what he was talking about. This could not be Persephone, beautiful daughter of Ceres, doomed to be the consort of Black Hades and live half her life in the Underworld as his Queen.

Persephone, also known as Goddess of Springtime. Yeah right! There was nothing in her demeanor that even implied she was the bringer of fresh clean rains, the one who raised the new crops from the land, and melted icy rivers.

The silence within the room hung like a nuclear cloud. Dangerous in more ways than one. Perhaps, it was dangerous to breathe? She had the air of a jealous and possessive wife, yet Julian's expression was bored at best.

"Evangeline and I are getting to know each other better." His words were innocuous enough, but Persephone didn't find them so. From the color of her face, Persephone felt he was betraying her by merely talking to someone else.

Possessive much?

"I can see that!" Topaz flashed and acid dripped. "Who is she?" Persephone flicked Evie a glance, gave her a fleeting once-over, then promptly dismissed her, not deigning to even meet her eyes. As if Evie were something to be scraped of her shoe.

"Oh, Evangeline? She is the new Ruler of the Underworld." Julian's cheek dimpled. He was enjoying needling his ex-consort. Enjoying it very much.

"What? Stop being stupid, Julian. I can't abide these jokes." She flicked her hand at him, ruby nails gleaming in the torchlight. Her cheeks remained rosy with frustration.

"Not a joke at all. I am being perfectly serious, Persephone. Evangeline had a bit of an accident and she is now the lady in charge." Julian sketched a bow and peeked at Persephone through thick lashes.

Persephone even managed to make the shocked expression on

her face look elegant and beautiful. She sat heavily on the edge of the nearest chair, holding onto the stuffed arm as if she was being swept away by a strong tide.

Evie stared at the goddess. Her reaction was a bit over-dramatic, but technically Persephone was now Evie's consort, and Evie was the one in control of Persephone.

Evie shivered at the thought. Hopefully Persephone would not turn the affections she'd lavished upon Julian onto her now that she was the big cheese.

Ick.

When Evie looked at Persephone, she didn't see much chance of that at all. The woman was devastated. Beautifully devastated. Tears filled her blue eyes, glittering on her lashes like tiny little diamonds. For the briefest of seconds, those eyes flicked at Evie and the angel shivered. If the stories she learned about Perse-phone—her nature and her purpose were actually God's truth—then this ain't the same Persephone.

The Goddess of the Seasons was a seasoned manipulator.

"Julian. Oh, dear god, Julian." Grief marred her features, tight-ening the lines in her face. She looked pretty good for her age. What? Three millennia, maybe more?

Evie raised her eyebrows at the object of Persephone's keen-ing. He shrugged, clearly as befuddled as Evie. "What's the matter now, Persephone? Don't you think you are being a bit over-dramatic?"

She rose and went to him, holding his hands in hers. "Julian, you don't understand. This means you are now mortal. You will die!" Then Persephone began to cry great big, hiccupping sobs. Evie wriggled in her seat. Julian cringed in her grasp as she fell against him still sobbing. He pushed her away and held her at arms' length.

"Persephone, get a hold of yourself. I was mortal to begin with." He spoke quietly and with intense calm. But Evie could tell from the strain at the corners of his eyes that he had realized what exactly Evie's change would mean for him.

Persephone's expression changed as she glanced back at Evie. "Well, who is she then? And how did she end up taking your place? How did she find all the Seals?" Persephone knew enough about the Seals to know how the transformation took place.

Evie shifted, uncomfortable as both Persephone and Julian regarded her. One stare cold and flinty, the other amused. Trust Julian to be amused at a time like this.

Evie caught herself short at the thought. What made her think she knew Julian at all? She certainly liked what she was looking at but that didn't mean anything. These people were strangers to her, and here she was lounging about while her friends still sat in the clutches of Marcellus. Those thoughts sobered Evie and she sat straight up.

When Julian didn't answer, Persephone glanced at him, venom flashing from her eyes. Some invisible battle waged between them, neither of them moving for a few moments. Evie held her breath and waited. At last the goddess took a step back, made a disgusted sound somewhere between a growl and a choke, turned on her heel, and left the room.

Evie watched the door as it shut behind the furious goddess. *This is so wrong. Persephone is a bitch?* Evie found she was actually upset at this newly discovered fact.

CHAPTER 21

*E*vie stared at the closed door, enjoying the almost awkward silence the goddess had left in her wake. Then she glanced at Julian and grinned. "Come, Julian, tell me more about you."

Julian smiled, awarding the closed door one glance of his own before taking a seat in a wide armchair. He picked up an overly large, well-worn book and seemed to fall straight into the text in a way that made Evie quite jealous.

"Come on," Evie urged. "I think it's pretty fascinating to be born at such an amazing time. So you have to tell me more. Otherwise, I might assume you are Caesar's son and that you knew Jesus personally." Evie smiled at Julian as he frowned at his book. But when he looked up, the pained expression on his regal face made her wonder if she'd been right.

Was it Caesar or Jesus he'd known?

"You are partly right, Evangeline. I am related to Caesar." Evie looked back at him so sharply she almost sprained her neck. "Close your mouth. You will catch flies."

"Silly." Evie laughed, waving her hand at him in a mock smack.

Odd for him to use such a familiar expression. "I don't think the Underworld possesses such things as flies."

"You'd be surprised."

Julian's enigmatic answer and the very heated look in his eyes as he stared at her lips made Evie feel slightly uncomfortable, so she shut her mouth and waited. She'd tried hard to stop thinking of home, so what better way than to concentrate on the hunky pin-up she was stuck with for the next month?

Nothing wrong with looking, nothing at all.

"Okay, where do I begin?"

"This may sound strange, but the beginning is usually the best place." Evie kept a straight face, but her eyebrow managed to curve of its own accord.

Julian grinned. "My mother was Julia Caesaris, daughter to Augustus Caesar." His eyes remained on Evie's face as she paled at his revelation. "I was her youngest child by Tiberius. Yes, he was the Emperor Tiberius, as you asked. I never knew my parents. My father's first wife, who also happened to be my mother's step-daughter, stole me away when I was an infant. She led everyone to believe I was dead. It was her way of dissolving the relationship between my parents. She wanted my father back. You see, my father so wanted to be Emperor he was willing to cast off the woman he loved for it. And Agrippina disliked my mother with a deep passion. Not only for marrying the man she loved, but for the way my mother treated her father."

Julian sighed, brushing his hand through his hair. "You see, everyone was a pawn. Everyone was used by someone. And Agrippina knew if I were to live in that household, I would be a pawn too. The only living grandchild of the Great Caesar. So she stole me away and replaced me with the body of a dead infant. One of the servants had just delivered a stillborn babe, and Agrippina saw her opportunity to give me a second chance at life. She swapped the babes and took me away to a wealthy family she knew. She cared enough to want to ensure I received a good education as well as a good life."

Evie was shocked at the words coming from Julian's mouth. Hard to believe that the young man she saw before her, so beautiful and strong, was actually the grandson and the son of emperors of Rome. He seemed far too down-to-Earth to be royalty. She wanted to hear more, wanted to ask a thousand questions. But she held her tongue. More because Julian's eyes held a faraway look that said he was in a place deep within his past. Filled with childhood wonder and memories of love and learning.

Evie's heart ached for the young boy taken away from his family by the arrogant God of the Underworld, to take his place while he was off god knows where, trying to find himself.

How hard was it for a god to find himself? And how long did it take, really?

"She came to see me, you know? I never knew it, only found out years later that she had visited with her friends regularly to see how I was doing. She often came bearing gifts and food. My foster-mother, Claudia, remained on good terms with Agrippina. She once said that Agrippina was a good woman at heart who had done a few wrong things in her life for the right reasons. I never knew what she meant until the history books and a few letters filled me in. You see, I was born in ten BC. I was twenty when Hades took me away. Julia was still alive and my real father, Tiberius, was Emperor. Perhaps it was a good thing Hades took me away. Who knows, I may have eventually succumbed to the typical Roman political maneuvering. Perhaps I may have tried to take the throne, may have succeeded had Agrippina ever admitted who I was. Not that I believed she would admit it. It would have defeated the purpose of everything she'd done."

Evie knew Julian would see the sorrow and sympathy on her face, but she didn't care. She watched his face as he spoke. "I had a blessed childhood. I was loved, healthy, well cared for. I could ask for no more than that. My foster father, Marcus, sent me away to school to be well educated. I must admit I was a rebellious and headstrong child. I was sent home from school. I was far too rambunctious to handle. Marcus relented and had me educated by his friend Horace."

Julian smiled when Evie's jaw dropped for the second time. "That's who you've been reading, isn't it?" She rose and picked up the book, flipping through the pages with extra care. The book looked ancient. "It's in Greek?" She raised her eyebrows in question.

"Horace wrote for me in at least five languages. It was his way of making me learn. I'd always thought they were stories, fictional tales to get me interested because they were always about a young and lonely boy or girl."

"Did he know your parents?"

"If you mean Tiberius and Julia, then yes. Even if he didn't know them personally, he moved in many circles that overlapped theirs."

"I bet. Wow, you knew Horace. And Virgil? And Ovid?" Julian nodded.

"Horace was my teacher for a while. And all three gave me many different lessons." Julian scrubbed his head again. "Horace died when I was nine. I was devastated. Little did I know that Hades had already chosen me. That Horace had a hand in the choosing."

Evie was silent, absorbing Julian's words. Was she really listening to the voice of a man from Horace's time? It should seem unbelievable, yet she believed him. She'd sunk back into the soft couch, and at some point she had curled her feet up under her, boots and all. Stricken, she sat up, putting her feet back on the ground where they belonged.

Julian laughed. "We don't stand on ceremony here, Evangeline. I want you to be comfortable while you are here." Then he closed his book and placed it on the arm of the chair again.

"Speaking of which, perhaps it is time to show you to your rooms."

Evie blinked. "My rooms? I have rooms?"

"Well, as the Ruler of the Underworld, it is befitting that you should have rooms. You can have mine, but I think you will be more comfortable with your own." Julian grinned as he teased her and she flushed. The door opened. "Evangeline, I'd like you to meet Pollo. Pollo, this is Evangeline, your new boss."

Evie listened to the steady clip-clop of what sounded distinctly like hooves as it moved from the stone at the entrance of the room to the carpet where it faltered at Julian's introduction but continued again, approaching her steadily.

A man came into her line of sight. Evie caught herself when she saw the horns, the sight of which drew her gaze downward to his legs—no, not legs, furred hindquarters and hooves. He was half a man and half a goat.

Evie blinked as he bowed before her. "A pleasure to meet you, my lady."

"Likewise, Pollo," was all she could manage as she swallowed and tried hard not to stare at the satyr.

"Pollo, please show Evangeline to the spare chambers."

The satyr nodded at the instruction without so much as a blink. "As you wish, my lord." Then he turned to Evie and inclined his head, his dark brown eyes kind and unassuming. "As soon as you are ready, my lady."

Evie sat up. "Oh, sure. I'm ready now." A bath and a nap sounded pretty good to her right now. She turned to leave when she remembered her bag. Evie glanced back at Julian. "I need a small favor."

Julian smiled, his eyes twinkling. "Name it."

"I need to go back to the room with the table. I left my bag there." She ran her fingers over her forearms, feeling an answering tingle beneath her skin, as if the dark tattoos knew she was thinking of them.

Julian's face darkened, and Evie felt a corresponding worry filter through her. "Of course. Pollo will take you." She was surprised he hadn't just said he'd have her bag brought to her. Instead, he'd given her permission to return to the room.

Evie followed a silent Pollo, who walked a few feet ahead, his pointed ears flicking every now and then as if he was listening up and down the tunnels for traffic. At last he slowed, and Evie recognized the inscribed mantel of the room in which she'd been ordained Queen of the Underworld.

Wordlessly, the satyr pushed open the heavy stone door and stood aside, allowing Evie to enter and retrieve her bag. As she hitched it on her shoulder, she glanced at the Seals.

Still embedded in the stone.

Pollo didn't even raise an eyebrow. Evie glanced at him as he closed the door and led her off, unperturbed.

Her mind ran in circles around medallions, Seals, and tattoos, so much so that when the satyr stopped to usher her into her room, she almost walked right into him. He stepped aside just in time and pretended she'd done nothing untoward, just gave her a small bow.

"Your rooms, my lady. Refreshments will be served in a few moments. Is there any particular food you prefer not to consume?"

"No, thank you, Pollo. I'm happy with anything." Evie nodded and Pollo bowed and left, closing the stone door softly behind him.

She had a sudden worrying thought as she studied the closed door. What kind of food would they serve down here in the Underworld? With a twist of her lips, she turned and shucked her bag onto the foot of the large four-poster bed.

Guess she would just have to wait and see.

Evie suddenly felt tired to the bone, an aching fatigue that seemed to want to drag her straight to her knees. Her thighs quivered and she sank onto the mattress, heaving a sigh. One that spoke of grief and loneliness, of vengeance and impatience, and of exhaustion.

She was about to allow her body to drop back onto the bed when she caught sight of tendrils of steam drifting from the wall in front of her. Her forehead scrunched and she rose, tiredness forgotten. She followed the steam around the wall and gasped.

Evie stood before a pool of water so clear she could see the stone floor and the seats carved out along the side walls. Steam rose from the surface and Evie bent to dip her fingers into the welcome warmth. She made her decision as soon as she felt the calming heat on her skin.

Within minutes, her clothing, weapons, and boots were off and she was soaking within the pool, giving no further thought to anything else but its soothing heat.

A COUPLE OF HOURS LATER, Evie sat on the bed, refreshed after a refreshing meal and a long nap. A light knock sounded on the door and a faun entered the room.

She paused just inside the room. "His Highness wishes to see you, Miss Evangeline." The girl sketched a quick curtsey, which Evie could see would be uncomfortable in her hoofed feet.

Hades had preferred the fauns as his servants, and as Evie could see, it remained the status quo. The faun smiled, although it appeared a mere courtesy as it never reached her eyes.

Guess she has chosen Persephone in this unspoken war.

Why she should have anything against Evie was a mystery, especially when Evie was adamant her stay would be as short as she could make it.

"What is your name?" Evie asked.

"Flavia, my lady."

"Thank you, Flavia. Where am I to meet him?" The faun hesitated, a cloud of confusion crossing her dull, brown eyes.

"Come, I will show you." She smiled and turned, her hooves making no sound on the carpet of moss.

Evie followed, glad she'd had a chance to eat and have a good nap before Julian thought to summon her. Why is he being so mysterious, anyway? Perhaps he had arranged a surprise? No. Evie shook head. It made no sense to presume what Julian's intentions were.

Flavia weaved through the warren of tunnels, this way and that until Evie was certain she'd never find her way back without help.

At last, Flavia stopped. "I have to leave you here. It's not far. Just follow the tunnel to the end. You will come to a large room."

Flavia stumbled a curtsey and left in a hurry. Evie stared at the disappearing faun in shock and disappointment. If she got lost inside these tunnels, no one would find her for days.

She turned to face the passage ahead and sighed. There wasn't much of a choice. Walk on or stand around helplessly like a fool.

The farther Evie walked down the passageway, the more she became certain that Flavia's message may not have been from Julian. Why would he want her to traipse around dark tunnels just to meet him? Either he had something pretty amazing to show her or she had just been royally duped.

Evie had her money on Persephone.

An archway on her left opened onto a small cavern. The entire floor of the room was a pool of dark water. Steam rose from the surface and a comfortable warmth exuded from the space. It would have made a marvelous hot tub had it not been for the floating splotches of red-hot flames which littered the surface.

Ouch.

Evie walked on, confident that this was not where Flavia had directed her. The smirk on the servant's face had alerted Evie to the possibility this was a hoax, but she could not assume it and ignore Julian's request. What if it was really Julian's request?

Evie passed another entrance to a large room on her right and then stopped in her tracks. Flavia had said to follow the passage until she came to the largest room. There she would find Julian.

None had been this large. None were this dark either. And it was the darkness which made Evie all the more nervous.

She entered the room slowly, searching for a torch to light up, anything to illuminate the room. A low rumbling echoed within the room, like the sound a fast-moving river made across a stretch of rapids, or the flowing of an underground river. The sound didn't concern her. She was seeing the depths of the Earth with a new light these days.

The room was large and airy, its ceiling higher than the entrance cavern. The acrid smell of burnt flesh lingered in the air along with the dry warmth of a burning fire. But no light shone within the cave, and though Evie could sense a solid presence in the room, she could see nothing yet. Not even a darker shadow to imply the presence of someone.

Even her angel-sight was doing nothing for her.

Evie hesitated, lingering just inside the threshold. When her lungs could no longer hold the air inside, she was forced to expel her breath. She'd been holding her breath in silent trepidation. Something within the room had begun to kindle fear deep within her gut.

A light flared in the corner, red flame flecked with yellow. Something large and angry raced at her with a roar that rippled around the room and entwined itself around her eardrums. The reverberations fed the fire of her fear.

Evie stumbled out of the room, but it was too late. Something long and scaled snaked out of the room and wrapped around her waist. It swung her back into the cave and tossed her straight onto the stone floor.

Evie tried to get up, but she was held firmly in place. In this position, she was unable to use her wings to flee, unable to free herself at all. She stared into the thick darkness. What fate lay ahead for her?

Slowly, Evie's eyes adjusted to the blackness and she managed to get a better picture of what it was that held her down, saw the enormous softly padded paw that held her down, the sharp-as-daggers claws that rested on her chest so near to Evie's heart that a deep breath would surely slice open her skin.

She lifted her chin to gaze into the eyes of a lioness whose golden pelt was both beautiful and astonishingly terrifying. The lioness's golden eyes scanned Evie, much like she would examine a carcass looking for the best place to rip it apart.

Prey. That's what Evie felt like.

The lioness bent her golden head to Evie and drew in a breath, sniffing at Evie's neck with interest. Evie felt the rush of warm air against her skin and tensed. She was paralyzed, unable to do much else besides wait for the crunch of teeth against bone.

None came.

The lioness continued to sniff her, butting her ear with a wet nose. Then Evie felt the seeking, scaly tail entwine itself around her leg and squeeze. Her eyes now fully adjusted to the darkness, and Evie took a deep breath, expecting to find it difficult with a huge lion's paw pressing down on her chest. But the paw had already been removed. And the owner of said paw walked around her, sniffing and staring.

It was then that Evie saw the head of a goat which sprung from the center of the lioness's back. She was face-to-face with a real live chimera. She got to her feet slowly, afraid to scare the chimera into an attack. She still circumnavigated Evie, seeming distressed. Evie's legs felt like rubber as she tested her weight, knowing she'd need to run when the creature next charged.

Her wings were ready to unfurl at any minute and Evie wasn't afraid to use them. The lioness's face was filled with sadness, while the goat stared at Evie with distrust. When Evie took a step toward the doorway, the lioness roared as if she was in deepest pain, and the goat bleated shrill and painful to Evie's ears.

It was the cacophony of animal sounds which stopped Evie from hearing someone approach.

The intruder rushed at her and in a breath, she was pushed gently against a wall. She gasped and looked up, ready to lash out at her attacker, when she met Julian's eyes.

"What are you doing here?" Julian face lay close to hers, worry creasing his brow. "Do you want to be killed?"

"Oh sure, it's so my favorite pastime," Evie said, swallowing hard. Her heart was beating a mile a minute at Julian's proximity—their bodies lay against each other touching from chest to hip.

The sound of her voice called to the tail of the chimera; it weaved, snaking through the air, attracted to Evie's voice. Julian moved in front of her and she felt strangely bereft. He guided her from the wall and walked backward with Evie behind him until they reached the safety of the passage.

"I was in no danger, you know."

"What exactly are you doing here?" Julian turned to Evie, an edge to his voice.

She backed away and ended up against the wall again. "Ask yourself that."

"What's that supposed to mean?" He took another step closer leaving not an inch of space between them.

Evie's breath came in short bursts. Her hands went to his chest and she felt the steady strong beat of his heart. She wanted to push him off but more than anything she wanted him closer.

Her body hummed with awareness, but she forced herself to concentrate on answering him. "Just that it was you who got me down here in the first place. If you're trying to kill me, I'm sure there are better ways than sending me to be chimera-chow."

"I didn't ask you to come here." Julian was frowning. The beating beneath her fingers sped up.

"Flavia said you did. Covering your tracks now, are you?" She raised an eyebrow, trying not to think about the heat that simmered between them. From Julian's rapid breath, it was clear he wasn't immune.

"Don't be silly. This reeks of Persephone."

When he spoke, his lips were so close she just had to lift her head a fraction of an inch for them to touch hers. The heated brush of his breath called to her. Instead, she remained motionless while trying to force her heart to return to a more decent rate. "I thought so too."

"Then why did you accuse me?" Julian glared at her, although she was sure she saw amusement in his eyes.

Evie lifted her chin, even though the action brought her mouth way too close to his. "How was I to know you wouldn't defend her and think I'm making all of this up? And how am I to be sure it wasn't really you in the first place?"

Evie's eyes narrowed as she met *his* eyes. He stared back at her, blinking so slowly, so lazily that she wondered how it was possible when his heart raced wildly beneath her fingers.

It was inevitable that their lips touched.

Evie breathed and leaned into Julian as his hands went around her waist. Just one kiss made her world turn on its head. They dragged apart just for air, while Julian took her lip between his teeth. Evie shivered as her body answered, her need hot and visceral.

"Julian." His lips took hers again. He kissed her deeply, wildly and she drowned in the intoxicating scent of him.

His lips released hers and he gripped his fingers into her hair, forcing them apart. "This isn't right." He shook his head and Evie watched him, a strange dread filling her. "No, don't look like that. This…you…it's perfect. But you are Hades now and *I* am mortal. And I'm dying. You have no idea what it's like to watch the people you love wither away and die right before your eyes. I just can't…"

Evie shook her head. She almost told him that she knew

exactly what it was like, but she didn't. She just leaned forward and kissed him.

Heat flared at her lips and he claimed her mouth, devouring her with a ferocious need. He kissed her, wild heated kisses filled with simmering need. His hands moved, slipped under her shirt. His fingers sizzled on her bare skin as he pressed her to him.

She wanted more and so did he, the need between them a blazing inferno. She moaned into his mouth and he kissed her harder, his hand moving to her breast, his thumb caressing sensitive skin.

And then he groaned and moved away, the air a cold blast of reality. Julian shook his head, his eyes one moment burning with need and the next black with iron fury. "Let's get out of here before I throw you to the chimera myself." Julian grabbed her arm and began to lead her out of the passage.

Evie pulled her elbow out of his grasp. Twin spots of anger rode high on her cheekbones. She hated being manhandled, especially right after he'd just kissed her senseless.

"Look, sorry." Julian held his hands up in surrender, his jaw tightening "I won't drag you there, okay? Just let's get out of here and find out exactly how you ended up here."

"Well, I have a feeling you won't need to look very far," Evie snapped, trying to get her emotions under control.

"If it *is* Persephone, she won't give up easily. You have to be careful, and not so trusting."

"I don't have to be anything. What I want to do is go home." Evie knew she sounded petulant, but at this point she didn't particularly care. She was tired and missed home too much. She had to watch her back, and now she had to watch her heart as well.

"Sorry, can't make that wish come true. The Binding holds you here for a month. No more, no less."

"No prizes for why it's called The Binding."

Evie kept her eyes off Julian as she walked. She had the

tendency to get all riled up over nothing just because she was looking at his face. She heard him chuckle and felt a tiny bit better. Enough that by the time they got back to the living area, she was considerably calmer and considerably less embarrassed.

"If you try to leave, it will keep you here forever, Evangeline." Julian's eyes were filled with worry. He'd been watching her.

Had he seen her emotional upheaval? Did he know he'd sent all her emotions into a frenzy with those heavenly kisses? Did he know her heart had broken for him?

Now she stared at him. She'd forgotten he was now mortal, and that he would begin to age. Something his body would not have experienced since he'd been brought here two thousand years ago.

"I thought I would be here forever. Never thought I would ever have the opportunity to return home."

"Do you ever go up?" Evie pointed upward to Earth-side, trying to keep the conversation light, trying to forget.

Julian nodded, his eyes shadowed. "I used to go, a long time ago. But when my parents died, I had no one to visit. What would I do up there?"

"Sightsee?"

"I see enough. One trip away shows me more about how awful people are to each other than I can handle."

"It's not that bad, you know." Evie tried and failed to make him feel better. It was clear he was weighed down by a melancholy that he couldn't shake.

And she wondered how much of it was her fault.

CHAPTER 22

Evie's run-in with the chimera, and Julian's super-sizzling kiss, stayed with her until the next day. She could not unravel her twisted emotions. So many things were so very wrong with her life.

She was accidentally Ruler of the Underworld, now stuck down in Hades for the next month, with no one for company but a too-hot-to-handle Julian and a bitter Persephone. Granted Cerberus provided her with some companionship, but it wasn't the same.

She missed her friends, missed home, missed her job too.

She did her best to avoid the company of the beautiful Persephone. Funny how the myths of the daughter of Ceres made her seem rather the damsel-in-distress. Nothing like the shrew she really was.

Evie cringed at the memory of her last run-in with the woman. Sure, Persephone had a problem with the fact her master was a woman. But it wasn't as if Evie was celebrating the fact.

So Sef had the hots for Julian. Evie had no intention on crashing that party. All she wanted was to get back home and find out how she was going to get Marcellus back for killing Patrick.

She did her best to avoid Julian too, her mind still a jumble of emotions when she thought of him and his lips and his body.

Evie shook her head then snorted. As if shaking her head would throw those thoughts out of it. It wouldn't work. Not when something deep inside her twisted with need every time she thought about Julian.

She found her feet taking her down the passageway into a part of the tunnels that she'd never been to before. She knew her way around enough not to be fazed by the new passages. Evie decided she would just enjoy the new places she saw while Julian was busy doing some earthquake management. Whatever that meant. He was still hedgy about what exactly he did when he disappeared so often.

The sound of water dripping onto stone rang clear as a bell through the tunnel. A shivering light called her to inspect the room up ahead. The walls were engraved with markings that glowed when she ran her fingertips over them.

Strange. That didn't happen around Julian's quarters. She made a note to double check when she got back.

A low groaning trailed the tunnel toward Evie. She hurried to the room and peered in. Not a good idea to go barging into dark places. The room was similar to so many other cells around here.

Only in this one, the walls and floor were covered in symbols which resembled the ones engraved on the Seals, and more importantly, like the ones on her arms. There were many more, and in so many combinations that Evie could tell the writer had told a story on the hard stone.

Her searching gaze found the source of the groaning.

There, in the center of the room, bound by chains which glowed red, as if living flames resided within each link, sat a man. Four chains bound him, each embedded deep within the ceiling, running along the floor and joining glowing brackets that hugged both wrists and ankles.

The man was filthy and haggard. Evie knew then and there that she would be doing something about the condition in which he lived. How could Julian allow this to happen? Prisoner or no prisoner, surely he deserved better. She had thought Julian would have more compassion than this.

Then she remembered where she was. Hades. Anyone imprisoned here, didn't get that way leading the perfect life. Who was he and what had he done?

When Evie stepped into the room, fire flared at her feet, sending her darting backward to avoid toasting her toes. Her gasp of surprise drew the man's attention away from his cupped palms to Evie's face.

When their eyes met, Evie was certain she'd seen a flash of emotion so deep it hurt for her to look at it. He rose to his feet, his movement so smooth and clean it was hard to believe he looked like he'd been confined to a cell with his movements restricted by so many chains.

Bits of dust drifted across the floor as Evie watched him. A feather grazed her cheek and Evie brushed it off her face unconsciously. She was so fascinated by this enigmatic man she remained fixed to the spot, waiting for him to speak. But she could not move farther into the room without being chargrilled.

"You should not be here," the man admonished her, which seemed incongruous as he stood clothed in rags and smeared with the dirt and sweat of days, if not months. It was a miracle the cell—there was no denying the man was a prisoner—didn't reek. Instead, there was a hint of frankincense in the air. Just a hint, and just enough to make Evie think it was her imagination.

He took several steps toward her then stopped, groaning again. He hunched over, his spine bent, his jaw clenched hard. A vein throbbed at his temple. All the signs she saw confirmed he was in incredible pain.

"Are you okay?" Evie asked. "Do you need help?"

"You should go. Leave me be." The man seemed intensely upset and desperate for Evie to leave.

"You're hurt. Can I call someone for you?"

"Bah. Call someone? So they can hurt me more?" His words held an edge of anger.

"Who did this to you? Let me speak to Julian—"

"What? Can you not see I'm a prisoner here?"

"Excuse me for trying to help." Evie's eyes narrowed at the man who did not even have the grace to be ashamed for his rudeness.

"I did not ask you for your help, did I?"

"Point taken. I will leave you to your solitude then."

It was possibly the word "solitude" that had been the straw that broke this prisoner's back because he looked about to apologize, or at least call her back. But at that moment, Pollo clacked in with another guard, possibly to check on the prisoner.

"Miss Evangeline! You should not be here." Evie turned to Pollo who stared at her—surprise and shock widening his eyes.

Evie thought she imagined the gasp she heard behind her. She glanced behind her at the prisoner who now had his head down. Perhaps he had hurt himself again, such was the depth of that intake of breath.

"I am fine, Pollo. I will return to keep the prisoner company."

"That might not be such a good idea, Miss Evangeline. I will have to check with His Lordship if it is okay."

"You go right ahead, Pollo. He is not going to change my mind."

This time the sound behind her sounded distinctly like a snigger. And this time, she did not look back. She turned and walked out of the room.

As she walked along the passage, a feather drifted onto her arm. Evie plucked it from her sleeve where it clung with static fingers. Holding it up to the light of a dismal torch, Evie was struck by its unique make-up. So beautiful.

And not unlike her own wings.

A wash of icy cold flowed over Evie as she turned on her heel and entered the room again.

This time, the prisoner had his back to the doorway. The neck of his ragged cloak was pulled down behind him to reveal his back all the way to the base of his spine. At the crown of each shoulder blade Evie saw the shattered, bloody remnants of a pair of wings.

Wings which looked like they had recently been hacked off. Congealed blood still clung to the shattered pieces of bone. Feathers stuck to the bloody gore that dotted the wound.

Evie's hand went to her mouth in horror. It did not stop her from crying in empathetic agony. What pain he would have endured when those beautiful things had been removed. Evie shuddered as the tears of horror slipped from her eyes. How could anything like this be condoned by Julian?

"Pollo, what is going on here?" Pollo stood at the prisoner's back, wiping the wounds and cleaning them. Hearing Evie's horrified voice, he turned and looked at her, his expression not unlike a little boy caught stealing cookies.

Guilty, but not sorry.

"I am doing my job, Miss Evangeline. That is what His Majesty will say too."

Evie, knowing it was better to stop banging her head against the brick wall of Pollo's stubbornness, turned and started down the passage.

"Wait."

The voice which spoke was gravelly and hesitant. Not Pollo's at all.

Evie returned to the room to see the abused and battered angel facing her.

"Julian cannot do anything about my wings or my incarceration." His voice echoed against the stone walls, gentle and soothing, as if his only care was to ease her pain.

"I would think he should be able to, considering *he* is the one keeping you here," Evie said dryly.

"It is not Julian who keeps me here. I have been here for almost a thousand years. And this is what I deserve." Now his voice held an edge of iron that frightened Evie. That seemed to reach deep into her heart and twist hard.

"Well, if you say you deserved it, then maybe you do, but I don't see why they need to mutilate you like this."

"They are not the ones doing it."

"Who is doing this to you then?" Evie frowned, confused.

"*I* am."

"What? Are you soft in the head or something?" Evie shook her head, a smile bordering on pity curving her lips.

"While I have my wings, I hear the bells of Heaven sing and it is more than I can bear." He sounded so sad that tears welled up in Evie's eyes without her even realizing. "When the wings are gone, I get some peace. When they grow back, I start to hear those bells again. The sound is so beautiful, I long for my home. It drives me insane."

"Er, you've got to be insane to do that to yourself. And look at the mess you make. Giving Pollo all this work."

Pollo raised his eyebrows in consternation. Evie was scolding the prisoner. "It's no trouble, Miss Evangeline. Gavriel is a good man although he had to take the punishment his God has commanded he receive. I am happy to tend his wounds."

"Well, Pollo, I hate to tell you this, but you belong in the loony bin right next to our de-winged friend, Gavriel, here." Evie could not understand how anyone, human or otherwise, would willing mutilate themselves like this. It was the same as cutting off one's arm. But neither Pollo nor Gavriel paid her any further attention.

"What did you do anyway? To end up here?"

"I disobeyed. You could say I chose the wrong side, or spoke my mind. It does not really matter now, does it?"

"Of course, it matters—even a one-year prison sentence must have a pretty good crime behind it for the law to hold it up. What did you do? Decimate entire cities? Kill innocent babes while they slept?"

Evie knew she was being a bit dramatic, but his situation was affecting her more than she expected it to. She was not sure why but this man's—no, this angel's—treatment made her incredibly angry.

"Who sent you here?" Evie demanded an answer, would not allow him to evade her probing.

"It was so judged by Heaven that I be sent here."

"God sent you here?" Evie asked, disbelief etched in the lines in her face.

"In a way, yes."

"Why would He do such a thing?"

"I fell in love," Gavriel responded with a tender smile lighting the craggy edges of his face.

Now that was a response she did not expect.

"Why would God punish anyone for love?" she asked, shaking her head.

"You could say that I defied my Father, and I had to pay the highest price for it."

"What price?"

"I fell from Heaven."

"More like thrown," Evie added dryly.

"That's one way of looking at it." Gavriel smiled and turned his head away.

Evie stared at Gavriel. She tried to force fresh breath through her lungs. It hurt to see those broken, bloody bones and torn wings whose feathers never ceased to float on the invisible currents of air which swirled within his cell. Hurt to imagine the agony Gavriel must have experienced, the deep and excruciating agony akin to having a limb cut off slowly.

And worst of all, it hurt to know he'd done that to himself.

Could the heavenly song be so agonizing for him that it would be necessary to hack those things of beauty off all by himself? Self-flagellation was not unheard of, but self-mutilation was a whole new ballgame for Evie to contemplate. Just the thought of holding a knife in her hand with the intention of carving off her wings was beyond imagining.

She backed away and leaned her weight against the wall beside the doorway, breathing hard. She had no energy to run. Even though that was what she wanted most. To be able to just run away from this place as fast as she possibly could.

She still had so many things to do. Her father was as elusive as ever. She'd lost the last lead on him centuries ago. But she forced herself to think about the here and now.

About the mutilated angel behind the wall.

She had two problems now. The pressure of her own wings at her shoulders bore her down as she empathized with the angel. And the weight of anger was pressing on her gut.

She was furious with Julian for participating in such a heinous activity—even after she reminded herself that Gavriel himself believed he deserved his punishment, but how could he when his reason was love? Evie glanced at the angel but Gavriel was shielded from her sight by Pollo as he cleaned the raw wounds.

She couldn't bear to watch anymore and turned to leave. But the carvings on the lintel caught her eye. Again, angelic script engraved deep into the stone. That was not unusual.

What made Evie's heart beat all the faster was the strange light that glowed within the engravings when she passed her fingers over them. As if her fingers gave the writing the power to glow from within the hard rock.

Her fingers lay against the rough stone as Evie contemplated its meaning. Just as she was about to withdraw her hand, a pulse of white-hot energy surged through it and travelled through her entire body.

She shuddered. Visions flitted through her mind's eye.

A valley spread below her, filled with bodies and blood and broken wings. A bright light bathed the bloodshed below, uncaring that such carnage should remain hidden.

Evie shut her eyes, but the vision did not cease.

Two warriors rose, battered and almost broken. They advanced on each other, circling, stepping over the bodies of fallen friends and comrades.

When their swords clashed, an almighty crash sounded through the valley and through Evie's mind and body. The sound was vicious thunder, roaring with anger. Evie wanted to block her ears. She was on her knees, unable to stop the sound from piercing her mind.

Light flashed, and the storm of the battle became more vicious.

As suddenly as it began, the vision ceased and Evie became aware she was on her knees, her forehead against the cool stone. She got up, her legs shivering, threatening to give way beneath her. She turned to see Gavriel and Pollo staring at her as if she'd just lost her mind.

How was she to tell them she suspected exactly that?

Before Pollo could leave his ministrations to check on Evie, she said a hasty good-bye to the pair and rushed out of the cell.

Evie stumbled through the tunnels to the rooms assigned to her. They were not very far away from both Julian's and Persephone's quarters, and Evie preferred neither of them were alerted to her presence for the moment—she could not bear the thought of a visitor.

Her head pounded, and the smallest bit of light hurt her eyes so badly that nausea gripped her. She retched as she opened her room door, then lifted her chin, hoping that would stem the rising tide. She leaned her head against the door and breathed rapidly until the tight band around her head began to release.

Evie lay down on her bed, deciding to rest and tackle the problem of Julian later. For now she needed rest.

Evie fell asleep and dreamed of angels battling to the death, of rivers of nectar running red with blood and a furious god who made the earth shiver with his anger.

CHAPTER 23

Restless, Evie went for a walk, allowing her feet to lead her and ended up in an auditorium. Carved out of the rock, the circular room could only have been modelled on the galleries of the Parthenon. The center of the room lay bare, awaiting its next occupants who would act out a scene from the Aeneid or the Iliad.

Evie sat on the highest level, close to the roof of the cave. She brought her knees to her chin and sat staring into space, desperately wanting to go home, desperately missing Patrick. But leaving meant she would forfeit the right to reverse the curse of those damned Seals.

That's what she thought of what the Seals had done to her. A curse. How did she hope to help her friends or the rest of the members of the Irin when she was stuck here?

Footsteps sounded in the hallway outside the auditorium. The long, slow, shuffling gait was so familiar that Evie's heart began to race in anticipation. But she tamped it down. It was hardly likely that Castor would be taking a stroll down the tunnels of Hades any time soon. Evie sighed and leaned her head on her knees glumly.

When Castor walked into the auditorium, she almost died with shock and joy.

"Castor." Evie rose and scrambled down the large steps. "Oh, you have no idea how happy I am to see you." Castor submitted to Evangeline's hugs and returned them with equal affection. "How are you? What happened after I left? Did Barry give you my message? What did Marcellus do when he found the Seals were gone?"

"Yes, Baa'ruk gave me your message. I was worried about you, so I am glad you sent him. And as for Marcellus, he is why I have come to find you, Angel."

Castor caressed Evie's hair and face, his eyes blank as his thoughts went to what he needed to say. Castor's pallid skin was lined with red whorls and lines, the curse of his demon blood. But it was his eyes which freaked most people out. Castor's pupils were a blood red, a sight that made the hair on most human's necks raise in bone-chilling fear. Evie couldn't understand that fear at all. Castor wouldn't hurt a fly.

"Marcellus...he doesn't know who helped you. He thought it was me. That's why I came."

A chill settled on Evie's chest. What had she done? "I'm so sorry, Castor. I put you in danger."

"No, Angel. Marcellus...he killed Father." Tears glinted in Castor's strange eyes.

Evie frowned and stared at the half-demon, curious now how he would know of the Master's involvement in Patrick's death. "How do you know that?"

But Castor's eyes remained a little out of focus and he shook his head. "He is a very bad man. Barry told me Marcellus wants to become Hades, Lord of the Underworld, and we have to stop him." Castor began to shake his head and looked much like he wouldn't stop. Evie knew this behavior. Had seen it many times before. He was agitated, worried, and grieving. And her heart ached for him.

She placed a palm on either side of his face and forced him to stop shaking his head. At last, he stopped and looked at her, his expression sad and forlorn. This is also what Marcellus had done—taken Patrick away from Castor and left him alone in the world.

For now, Castor had to focus on why he'd come. And how he'd gotten here.

"Baa'ruk helped you get here, didn't he?"

"Yes. He was good to me. Showed me where the cave was and told me to take the coin for the boatman and he told me to take something of yours with me. He was right, Angel. The big scary dog smelled your scarf and let me go through."

Evie was so grateful to have someone familiar with her that she didn't care how Castor got there. But she did care what Marcellus was up to. "Come. Tell me about Marcellus." Evie sat down and patted the stone seat next to her.

Castor sat heavily, massaged his club foot, and sighed. Evie's heart ached to think he'd walked all that way just to find her.

"Marcellus knows how to enter the Underworld. And now that he has discovered the Seals are gone, he is furious. He searched everywhere. And he thinks it was me that took them. He burned my house, Angel."

Castor fell forward into Evie's arms, tears seeping from his red-rimmed eyes. Evie gasped, shocked. Tears built up in her throat and threatened to overflow. Castor's house was his most special place; it gave him a purpose and a meaning to his life.

He had lived most of his life in solitude. Most people gave him a wide berth, and more people just didn't have the time for him. How could Marcellus do such a thing? It seemed he was as thoughtless and evil as Evie had suspected.

Evie cradled the half-demon in her arms as he grieved for the loss of his home. "So what is Marcellus doing now?" she asked, more to distract Castor than anything else.

"He is coming to find you, Angel." Castor sat up and stared at Evie with wet eyes. "He is coming to Hades."

How did Marcellus know I took the Seals? How did he know where I was? Evie's mind went to the dark creature that had lurked within the shadows of Marcellus' office. It made sense that the Master would know more than he should, considering he had the help of dark magic.

"Let him come, Castor. There is nothing he can do to me," Evie assured him, but Castor shook his head urgently.

"He is coming to take back the Seals."

"Castor, don't worry. Even if he takes the Seals, there is nothing he can do to make himself Hades, at least not for the next month."

"So you are safe?" He stared at her, eyes filled with worry.

"Yes, dear Castor. You need not worry about me." At least not for now. "Now, there is something you need to know."

"What is it, Angel?" he whispered.

"Two things, Castor. One. Please do not mention the Nephilim to anyone while you are here in the Underworld. Do you understand?" Castor nodded, his face serious. "Two—something happened when I brought the Seals to Hades. An accident, Castor. The Seals made me the ruler of the Underworld."

Castor uttered a cry of horror, bringing both hands to his mouth. "Oh no. Angel, you cannot be Hades. A Nephilim as the Ruler of the Underworld? If they find out, they might kill you." Castor still whispered. Horror lurked in his voice.

"Don't worry. Nobody knows, and I have no intention of telling anyone."

"Telling anyone what?" Julian stood in the doorway, his eyes dark and watchful, making her think of something dangerous.

Something lethal.

He'd overheard the last bit of their conversation and Evie had no idea how to get out of answering his question. There was an uncomfortable pause in which Evie flailed around for something to say.

"About me." Castor stood up and drew the hood of his cloak off his head to reveal his face in the weak light of the auditorium. Julian met his eyes, and Evie was glad to see his expression did not reflect disgust or dislike in any way. Glad he was the type of person she would happily associate with. "I do not wish for anyone to know about my bloodline. Is it not true that demons are not welcome here in the Underworld?"

Julian shook his head in disagreement. "It is clear you are not a full demon, Castor. Thus, there is none who can claim you are demon for you are half human too." Julian met Evie's eyes over Castor's head and smiled in understanding.

Evie, although relieved, felt a spasm of guilt. She gave Julian a grateful nod and lowered her head as she supported Castor, walking with him across the uneven stone floor of the gallery toward Julian. He surprised her again by taking Castor by the forearm, an ancient respectful greeting that had the half-demon's eyes widen in surprise and pleasure.

"Castor, know that you are as welcome here as Evangeline is. This is your home and you are safe here. Whatever your needs, they will be met." Julian's tone was firm, as if someone was listening.

Then, Julian walked to the doorway and leaned outside. He called out to someone, probably one of his wait-staff, Evie suspected. Seconds later a short, wiry faun trotted to Julian and leaned forward to catch his master's instructions. He glanced as Castor with curious eyes, then beckoned to the half-demon.

Castor glanced at Evie, frowning. She patted his arm. "Don't worry. Go with him. He'll look after you." When Castor didn't move, she gave him a small shove. "Go on. You'll be safe. Right, Julian?" She looked over at Julian who nodded and smiled.

At last, Castor seemed convinced. His frown relaxed a little and he followed the faun. At the door he paused, a look of fear filling his eyes. "Evie? What about Marcellus?"

Evie smiled, hiding the hard edge to her anger. "Don't worry about Marcellus. I'll deal with him."

Castor smiled, apparently satisfied that Evie would fix everything. And he and the faun disappeared down the passage.

"So, who is Castor?" Julian asked after a short silence.

For a moment Evie wanted to refuse to talk about Castor—her protective instinct kicking in automatically, but what would be the use? Besides, she'd seen the understanding and acceptance in Julian's eyes.

"He is one of my mentor's charges. Castor was born to a human woman. She discarded the child when she discovered what he was. Patrick took him in and brought him up as one of his own. Now the new head of my organization—the one who wants the Seals—thinks that Castor had something to do with them disappearing from his office."

"But *you* stole them from his office." Julian laughed, his eyes sparkling and oh-so-sexy. "You know, you would have done well in the Roman Army. No doubt you would have been the first female general in the history of the Roman Army."

Evie liked Julian's smile, and she smiled back. Only, on the inside she was no longer smiling. A deep sadness entwined itself around her heart, threading itself through her soul. She had made Julian mortal and it was all because of her own stupidity. Her own foolish need to be a heroine and stop Marcellus.

And so, she had sentenced Julian to death.

Evie's own immortality would not be jeopardized whether she was ruler of Hades or not. But in Julian's case, Persephone was right. This was the beginning of the end of Julian's life. From the day she took his place, he would grow old. And if Evie was unable to find a way to get herself out of the imprisonment of the job of King of the Underworld, she would be sentenced to watch the beautiful Julian age day by day, only to see him die.

Evie grieved somewhere deep inside herself ,where tears could not express her deepest emotion.

"So when do you expect to see this Master of yours?"

"No idea. Castor means well. But he can be unclear at times. He is a bit simple-minded but he's also fairly competent." Evie eyed Julian, trying not to think of the both of them in certain compromising positions. "Why are you so accepting of him?"

"I am a Roman," Julian answered simply, his eyes not leaving her face. "When I was growing up, there were many lepers on the streets and leprosy sometimes appeared among the slaves. Even among the wealthy too. One of the servants in Marcus's household contracted the disease. He was a playmate of mine. And I was with him until his last hour. Even when Claudia forbade me from seeing him, I still went. I had no understanding of the disease then. Only later did I realize how I had endangered my own health. The experience taught me to appreciate the suffering and needs of those less fortunate."

I nodded at Julian, understanding a little more now of what Julian Ceasaris was about.

CHAPTER 24

As soon as Julian left the auditorium Evie hurried to her room. Marcellus would not be far behind Castor. Knowing him, he would have had Castor followed. She needed to be ready for him. She shut the door, her heart thudding at the prospect of meeting Marcellus head on in a fight. But from what Castor had said she didn't seem to have any other choice.

The Master was coming to Hades to get her.

She rummaged through her bag and strapped on her weapons. At last she grabbed her sword and rang her bell for service. A faun arrived within minutes, leaving hurriedly with a message from her to Castor to meet her in her room.

Minutes later, Castor arrived out of breath. "You didn't have to run, Castor," she said gently.

"But your message said it was urgent," he answered simply, an expression of dismay darkening his demon coloring.

Evie smiled. "That's all right, Castor. You did fine." Evie tucked her hand into his and drew him to the doorway. "Now, come with me. I have someone I think you would like to meet."

Evie led Castor all the way to the entrance to the Underworld. Chains clinked in the cave and the sound of ragged breathing reached their ears. The three-headed dog jumped forward, lowering himself on his forepaws, wagging his tail and staring at Castor.

Castor let out a shout of laughter at seeing Cerberus again and went straight to him. "Castor, this is Cerberus. Cerberus, this is my friend Castor. Make sure you look after him." The gigantic dog stared at Evie and snuffed as if agreeing to her instruction.

After they were properly introduced, Evie said, "Castor, I need you to do something for me."

Castor turned to her, a huge grin on his face as he rubbed the ears of one of the dogs while another head licked the side of his face. The third whined, clearly unhappy that he couldn't get to Castor.

Evie shuddered and prayed they wouldn't lick him to death. "I need you to take Cerberus into the tunnel. Just a little bit away from here so I don't disturb him."

Castor nodded and obeyed without question, taking the dog away from the entrance to Hades. Castor had a way with animals and it seemed he was just as good with the three-headed monster. Evie had to admit the creature had wormed its way into her own affections too.

Now Evie stood at the center of the cavern, waiting for Marcellus. The air was cool on her face, as if it knew she was overheated with thoughts of anger and revenge. But it was unable to douse the fire and rage inside her.

She stood stock still, hand at her weapons, staring into the dark maw of the tunnel leading to Cerberus, waiting for the treacherous creep to arrive. She had come prepared, strapped with her scimitar and her daggers. And she had even brought her short-sword, carrying it at her waist just in case.

Hatred built within Evie, overflowing as her mind focused on the burning fact that Marcellus was responsible for the death of her beloved father and mentor. Her heart thudded against her ribs as fury sent blood rushing through her veins.

Faint sounds travelled to her through the warren of the passages. Booted feet splashed into small streams of water, rushing toward her. Somebody was making their way down the tunnels toward her. Someone who had brought company.

If it was Marcellus she was more than ready for him.

At last, the darkness blended together into the diminutive shape of Marcellus as he walked toward Evie, so confident, so arrogant. His contingent of guards followed, gathering behind him, ready to fight his battles for him.

Coward.

"Ah, Evangeline. I didn't expect to find you so easily." He looked around, made a face of distaste before his eyes alighted on her again. "Nice place you found to hide out in."

"Thought you would appreciate a welcome party." Evie strengthened her stance, clenching thigh and arm muscles in anticipation of kicking his sorry ass.

His face darkened with anger, his eyes narrowing on Evie's face. "You know what I'm here for, Evangeline. Now, hand over my Seals." Marcellus had the gall to open his palm and waggle his fingers at Evie.

She was barely able to keep herself from laughing at him. Instead, she shook her head and answered him coldly. "Even if I do, they won't do you much good." The Seals were still tightly set into the stone table and would remain right there until her twenty-eight days were over.

Not something she planned on telling Marcellus though.

"Why is that?" Marcellus moved slowly, his boots rasping on the stone floor as he circled Evie. She kept her eyes on him as he went. A vein throbbed at his temple. "What have you done with my Seals?"

"I haven't done anything with them. The Seals have chosen the new Ruler of the Underworld all by themselves."

"Really? I don't think I believe you, my dear. You cannot think

I'm that gullible. Do you really think I will listen to you prattle and leave that easily?"

Evie tugged her sleeve up and thrust her forearm at Marcellus. His eyes widened and he double-stepped backward to avoid being punched. The script on her arm began to glow, iridescent gold. At the same time, the faint chimes of the Seals rang around the chamber, racing down the tunnels and returning on the echoes.

Marcellus straightened in shock, his face eked of all blood. "What have you done?" His entire body vibrated with fury. Marcellus roared, spittle flying from his mouth as he closed in on her. His rage contained a volatile violence that made her shiver. "You have no idea what you have done.... What you've done to me." Marcellus, his fury taking control, lunged for Evie.

He hadn't planned his strategy well and Evie saw her opportunity and swung backward, side-swiping him across his face with the hilt of her sword. The short man went sprawling and sliding across the stone floor coming to a stop in an undignified heap against the far wall.

He lifted his head, putting his hand to his lip and staring furiously at the blood. "Get her, you imbeciles!" He screamed at his guards, who were still standing and watching, not interfering in the least.

Now, they advanced in unison, their swords at the ready. Evie sank lower on her knees, finding her center of gravity, weighing the sword within her hand. She waited. Six against one was not an even fight. But Evie had been trained well. They were clumsy and afraid. Easy pickings.

Because even *six* human Irin Warriors against one Nephilim was a fight favoring the Nephilim.

Although she knew she was taking a huge chance, Evie let her wings burst through. White and silver feathers flapped out behind her and filled the room. Silver dust floated daintily to the ground every time her wings shuddered behind her. Evie's wingspan rose twice her height and just a flick of a single wing sent two of Marcellus' guards tumbling into the stone walls, out like the proverbial light.

Two down, four to go.

They circled, their eyes hard and predatory, while Marcellus sat back and wiped more blood from his lip. His face was filled with malice and an expression of victory he was likely to regret soon. Perhaps it was her youthful looks and demeanor that made him forget her experience in combat. She preferred to leave him to his ignorance.

They came again in one wave and Evie was forced to launch herself into the air. She hovered above them for a moment, watching them, feeling her skin tingle, knowing the tattoos would be glowing golden. She could see the fear in their eyes.

Most humans feared or revered the Nephilim and Marcellus' lackeys stank of fear. Evie drew her sword as she hovered over them. A sword-wielding angel would be a terrifying sight. She smiled coldly as all four guards fled to the sound of their master's curses.

Evie turned to Marcellus who had risen, his hand fisted, his anger still almost palpable, his diminutive state even more prominent from her height.

"Marcellus, you have done enough damage to the Brotherhood." Evie advanced on him and he backed away.

Marcellus turned and raced down the tunnel directly behind him with Evie close on his heels. He was so predictable. She had known he would run.

Evie guided his flight down long passages until he almost reached his destination. She kept a bead on him up ahead as he almost entered an empty cave on his left. Marcellus stared inside the room, then sent a furtive look back down the passage in Evie's direction, a deer-in-the-headlights expression paralyzing the muscles of his face.

She wasn't going anywhere, and he knew it. He turned and

gave her one last desperate glance before stumbling into the next cave entrance.

Evie heard the groan and sneeze of the disturbed creature within the darkness. The chimera must have been close to the entrance, clearly visible to Marcellus. The back of his head and coat came into view as he began to edge out slowly, dragging in his next breath. Then he stopped dead.

She heard the silence which followed in which she imagined Marcellus and his executioner staring each other down, one in fear, the other in lip-smacking anticipation. Then she heard Marcellus' fear-filled scream. She listened with a hardened heart to the sounds emanating from the cave as the chimera tore him to pieces.

And while she listened, her eyes filled with tears as her life with Patrick played before her eyes, as his love filled her heart. As she remembered his hand in her life, his guidance and the years of training and teaching he had invested in her.

She still had to find a way out of Hades, still had to figure out how to restore Julian's immortality.

And then there was Daniel.

And not forgetting the whole Ruler-of-the-Underworld thing —no way could she accept that role, which meant finding a way to reverse it.

But for now, she was at peace.

~ TO BE CONTINUED ~

Want to read what's next in the Irin Chronicles series?
Requiem

ACKNOWLEDGMENTS

To my support structure - the Inklings and the Indie Inked ladies- without whom I think I would be more than a little lost!
To my editor Tracy Riva and my proofreader Karen Mead, thank you for working so hard to make Retribution that much more amazing.
To my family – I'm not entirely sure what I would do without you guys. Please don't stop taking care of me.
To Kate Strawbridge- my amazing friend and super-talented cover artist. You have magic fingers and magic eyes!
And to my readers. Don't stop reading…

ABOUT THE AUTHOR

I have been a writer from the time I was old enough to recognize that reading was a doorway into my imagination. Poetry was my first foray into the art of the written word. Books were my best friends, my escape, my haven. I am essentially a recluse but this part of my personality is impossible to practice given I have two teenage daughters, who are actually my friends, my tea-makers, my confidantes… I am blessed with a husband who has left me for golf. It's a fair trade as I have left him for writing. We are both passionate supporters of each other's loves – it works wonderfully…

My heart is currently broken in two. One half resides in South Africa where my old roots still remain, and my heart still longs for the endless beaches and the smell of moist soil after a summer downpour. My love for Ma Afrika will never fade. The other half of me has been transplanted to the Land of the Long White Cloud. The land of the Taniwha, beautiful Maraes, and volcanoes. The land of green, pure beauty that truly inspires. And because I am so torn between these two lands – I shall forever remain cross-eyed.

Stalk Tee here:
www.tgayer.com
tee@tgayer.com

facebook.com/TGAyerAuthor

twitter.com/TGAyerAuthor

bookbub.com/profile/t-g-ayer